DESTINY OF THE WOLF

PACK LOYALTY

BOOK THREE

AMELIA SHAW

CHAPTER 1
KARA

I was on edge today. Not for any reason I could put my finger on. The atmosphere around me, inside me, just felt tense, like the air before a storm.

Across from me, on the other side of the lawn, the pack Alpha, Allara, sat with her feet up, watching over the children running about. Although her body language was lazy, I could tell that she was on alert in the way that Alphas always were, scanning for threats over at the tree line and ensuring the safety of pack members, even while appearing relaxed.

Not that she could spring into action right now, though, even if something did turn up to threaten us. Not in her condition. The sundress she wore couldn't hide her large, round belly. She chewed her bottom lip, deep in thought over something.

Reid, her mate, crossed the lawn to join her, carrying two large glasses of lemonade. Allara accepted one, smiling up at him with a softness she reserved only for him. He bent his head to press a kiss to her lips. His fingers were gentle as they slid through her hair. The way he treated her—as if she were made of glass and the most precious thing on earth—was surprising for such a big man.

Bitterness spiked through my chest and it only took me a second to realize what the feeling was.

Envy.

As Reid and Allara got to talking, I bent my head back over my needlework and tried to shake away the feeling.

Those two had always known they were fated to be together. Ever since we were kids. Back then it had made us all laugh, the way they were with each other.

Not now. Now, it made us all yearn for something similar to what they had.

Unlike Allara and Reid, though, I'd never had even an inkling of that feeling toward anyone in the pack. I'd never experienced the pull they all talked about. That unshakable certainty that *this* shifter was the one for me.

So, I kept to myself. The other members of the pack didn't bother with me, which suited me just fine. It ran both ways; most of the time, I was happy enough in my own company.

Since my brother Jason had found his mate Tammy, I'd withdrawn even more. It wasn't anyone's fault I didn't feel right in company anymore. Besides, it meant I had more time to work on my art. I should be happy about that.

I smoothed a hand over the pattern I was working on: dozens of trees embroidered in shades of green. The forest scene would eventually become part of a quilt for Allara's baby. The room they had planned for him, or her, was spectacular.

Yeah. I have all I need, right here.

Allara and Reid were still deep in conversation. Even from this distance, I could see they were arguing about something. Allara's brow creased. It was an expression I knew well.

She doesn't want to hear whatever he's saying, but she knows he's right.

Sure enough, a few moments later, Allara threw up her hands.

Fine, fine.

Reid sat back, satisfied, and I smothered a laugh. Allara wasn't one to lose a fight and she wouldn't take it well. Reid brushed his hand against hers, and she relented, tangling their fingers together. Like all their disagreements, it was over before it had really started.

I shook my head and returned to my embroidery.

Kids on the lawn played under the watchful eye of half a dozen shifters. Beyond the grass, a group of pack members emerged from the trees carrying a deer between them. No one would go hungry tonight.

At the other end of the village, the vegetable garden was blooming; come Fall, we would be laden with fresh fruit and vegetables.

Everything was exactly as it should be. And yet, there was something I couldn't put my finger on... Why did I feel so unsettled?

Is it my imagination, or can I smell a storm on the horizon?

It was late evening by the time Allara and I were alone and we could catch up properly. We sat on her porch together drinking iced tea and listening to the cicadas flitting in and out of the grass around the house.

Allara had one hand on her belly, and the other absently stirred her drink.

"It's any day now, Kara." She patted her stomach and grinned. "Ugh, I'm so *done* being pregnant."

I chuckled as I remembered how Tammy had gotten in the weeks leading up to her due date. Jason had been almost as bad as his partner, fussing over Tammy and the imminent event as if everything else in the world had come to a stop. Which I guess, for my brother and his mate, it had.

Setting foot in that house was like waiting for a bomb to go off toward the end. By the time baby Mae finally arrived, we were all at our wits' end, only to be greeted with the most placid, easy-going kid ever.

Not for the first time, I wondered what Reid and Allara's baby would be like. I took a sip of tea, hiding a little grin. Whether male or female, the coming bub was bound to be a leader of some kind. "How's Reid holding up?"

Allara shrugged. A smile played about the corners of her mouth. "Put it this way, I'm gonna miss having him wait on me hand and foot. Though it has started to get a little ridiculous—he carried me into the *bath* yesterday. Like, actually ran me a bath and *put* me in it."

We both laughed aloud this time. How well Reid treated his mate came as no surprise to me. Few men looked at a woman the way Reid looked at Allara.

Her smile slowly faded, and her eyebrows pinched together. "Honestly, I'm frustrated. Until this baby is born, I'm stranded here. It makes my business as Alpha kind of limiting."

"Yeah." I put a comforting hand on her arm. "I can imagine."

It wasn't a situation an Alpha typically found themselves in, especially since most wolf shifter Alphas were male. As much as Allara had flourished in her role as pack leader, she now had a new priority: motherhood.

"I'm gonna confess something..." Allara turned to me, setting her drink down on a table next to her.

Her expression was serious, so I mirrored her posture.

"This isn't purely a social visit. I need to ask you a favour."

"Oh?"

Allara and I had been best friends since we were kids. We'd reconnected almost immediately after she'd returned to the pack, picking up right where we left off. The fact she was now my Alpha hadn't changed that relationship between us. There was little I would refuse her.

"I've been in contact with Elder Frey, from the Thornwood Clan. He's been keeping things running round those parts, ever since..." Allara's face twisted with discomfort. "Well, you know."

Right. Their Alpha's passing.

I'd never met the Thornwood Alpha face to face, but over the years he'd nurtured an alliance with Allara's father. News of his sudden, recent death had spread like wildfire to every shifter pack in the state.

Shifter packs fiercely guarded their secrets, especially upon the death of an Alpha. The risk for any pack was greatest just after an Alpha passed, and before the new leader was chosen. But the Thornwoods had been in open disarray for months now.

"They haven't chosen a new leader yet?" I couldn't keep the shock out of my voice. I'd never heard of such a thing—a pack running wild for so long with no sworn Alpha. How had they survived a takeover bid?

Allara's face darkened. "Oh, they had chosen one. The Thornwood Alpha's son was all set to inherit, but for some reason, on the day he was set to be sworn in, he took off."

"He... what?"

"He ran off somewhere." Allara looked *pissed*, and I sensed it wasn't a good idea to point out right this minute that *she* hadn't embraced the role of Alpha with open arms at first, either. Instead, I tried to keep my face totally blank of emotion.

"The truth is," Allara continued, hefting herself back in her chair with a heavy sigh, "I'm worried. Jaime's still out there, and the Thornwood pack—the one closest to our borders—currently has no Alpha. Honestly, I don't know what Jaime's capable of. If he stepped in and took over..."

I caught a flicker of real fear in her expression.

I shared her fear. Jaime was unstable and if he stirred up trouble with our nearest neighbor, that trouble could spill over to us. I stared out at the clearing in front of us. Earlier that day, it had been full of kids playing chase, giggling and play-fighting with each other.

The thick line of trees at the edge of the grass seemed darker than usual, full of shadows. I knew it was simply my mind playing tricks, but it felt like danger could be lurking around every tree trunk or branch.

I shook the thought away.

"So, what does this have to do with me?" I asked.

"Reid is going to meet with the Thornwood Clan," Allara said. "Normally, I'd go with him, but I don't feel strong enough at the moment. I want you to go in my place."

I stared at her, shocked. *"What?* Why me?"

"Because I trust you," Allara said simply. "And I don't say that about many people. I need people I can trust right now. Your brother and Tammy are busy with Mae, and besides, you were my first choice."

She smiled and squeezed my hand.

"But..." I fumbled. "I don't know anything about politics!"

It might have sounded like a feeble excuse, but it was true.

I wasn't like Allara—bold, confident and strong. She'd left our village without a backward glance and lived for years in a strange city before returning to take up the role of pack leader. She was born for it. I'd always been content to spend my days here with my weaving and craftwork, making beautiful things for my community.

I couldn't just step into her role next to Reid and do the job well. I didn't believe in myself that much, and I was positive no one else would, either. There was no way I could do it.

"Kara." Allara caught my eye and held it in that instinctive, unyielding way that only an Alpha could. Damn. When she pinned me with *that* look, I knew I wouldn't be able to refuse. "Look at me," she insisted. "I *know* you can do this. I wouldn't have asked you otherwise."

I opened my mouth and closed it a few times, discarding excuses that I knew she'd throw aside as soon as I uttered them out loud.

What if I messed up? One wrong move could wreck whatever alliance Allara wanted to build and make things worse for *both* clans.

But the look on her face told me that I couldn't argue. Allara had already made up her mind. More than that, I could hardly disobey a direct order from my Alpha.

"Fine. When do we leave?" I mumbled.

Allara brightened immediately. She sat back in her chair, looking like a weight had been taken off her shoulders.

At least she's confident. That makes one of us.

"Tomorrow."

So soon? I almost squeaked. Allara caught my expression anyway and draped an arm around my shoulders, squeezing tight.

"You'll be perfect, Kara." A soft smile played around the corners of her mouth. "You'll see."

It was still dark outside when my alarm started blaring, far louder than I expected it to be.

With a groan, I gave it a couple of smacks to turn it off. I rolled over, every muscle in my body tensed, and listened with bated breath for the sound of a baby crying. Had my alarm woken Mae?

There was nothing but silence from the rest of the house. I let out a long sigh of relief and allowed myself to relax into my pillows.

Tammy would never forgive me if I woke Mae up with my stupid alarm.

On the chair beneath the window, the bag I'd packed yesterday lay in wait. I glowered at it, but it didn't burst into flames. It remained exactly where it was, mocking me. Ready to leave.

With a heavy sigh, I knew I couldn't delay any longer. I clambered out of bed and threw on my clothes. I was meeting Reid outside in half an hour. I had just enough time to eat some toast and brush my teeth before he'd be here.

There was no point waking Jason and Tammy. I'd said my goodbyes to them yesterday, and with Mae well and truly making her beautiful presence felt, like all babies do, the sleep-deprived parents needed as much rest as they could get.

Tammy had hugged me tearfully and asked when we were coming back. She didn't need a shifter's advanced senses to pick up on the tense atmosphere. Jason had not said anything, but his body language when he moved in for a hug and the way he'd squeezed me so hard my feet lifted off the floor, told me how worried he was about me going on this mission for Allara. Jason was more than a big brother to me. Since Mom and Dad had died, we were all the family we had left.

Once I had my bag on my shoulder, I glanced out the window and into the dark street. I could see Reid heading toward our house in the dim light cast by the street lamps. Tension was written across the broad line of his shoulders.

I didn't blame him. My own shoulders were tight with apprehension. I knew this mission wasn't his first choice, either. He'd much rather be with Allara and his unborn child right now. Like any expectant dad, he wanted to be around just in case Allara went in labor earlier than expected.

Sometimes pack duty has to come first.

I tip-toed down the stairs and shut the front door behind me as quietly as I could. Reid nodded as I came down the front steps of the house and gestured for me to follow him.

"Morning Kara. C'mon." He hitched up his own bag on his shoulder as I fell into step beside him. "Truck's all packed and ready to go."

I stowed my bag in the bed of his truck and climbed into the passenger seat, trying not to feel awkward. It wasn't often that Reid and I were in each other's presence without Allara. I was hoping we'd find things to talk about along the way, and not spend the whole trip in quiet discomfort.

If he sensed any of my awkward feelings, he didn't show it. He looked a million miles away as he turned the key in the ignition and we headed down the road that led out of the village. There were dark circles under his eyes, like he hadn't slept in a month.

He glanced at me properly once we were on the main road. "All good?"

I nodded. "Sure." I must have sounded unconvincing, because he grinned briefly.

"We'll be back before you know it, Kara. All will be well."

Judging from his expression, I could tell he wanted to believe that just as much as I did. This trip was the last thing either of us wanted to be doing right now. But orders were orders, whether you were the Alpha's friend, or their mate.

The trees rushed past as we drove. The sun began to rise, and golden light dappled the hood of the car. I tilted my head up, looking through the sunroof at the crows circling high overhead.

"What are they like?" I eventually asked, breaking the comfortable silence.

"Who? The crows?" He followed my gaze upward, then concentrated back on the road again.

I rolled my eyes and looked directly at him. "No. The Thornwood Clan, of course."

Reid drummed his fingers against the steering wheel. "Oh, ya know."

"No, I *don't*." I frowned out at the road ahead. "It's a genuine question, Reid. I've never even been to the other side of the creek."

Reid's brows shot up. "I didn't realize."

I could see he was turning my question over in his mind, trying to find the right words. "They're... secretive," he said eventually. "They keep to themselves, you know? The same as any shifter pack."

Huh. That wasn't much to go on.

We fell into silence for a few more miles until eventually, Reid spoke up again.

"You know Naomi, right? She's one of the Thornwood Clan. Or she used to be, anyway." He shrugged. "Who knows where she's at, these days."

I wrinkled my nose. Of course, I knew Naomi, and I have to admit, I really did not like her. My brother's on-again, off-again ex. In the old days, she'd stick around just long enough to mark her territory and get Jason hooked on her before prancing off again. She reminded me of a poisonous flower: lovely to look at, but you didn't want to get too close.

When Tammy had entered the picture, I wasn't the only one in our clan to breathe a sigh of relief. Naomi had scampered away once she realized Jason wasn't coming back to her. I didn't know where she was, now, and frankly, I didn't care, as long as she stayed away from my little family.

Reid caught my scowl and broke into laughter. "Aw, c'mon! You can't judge a whole clan by one wolf, Kara."

I made a noncommittal noise and crossed my arms. "Fine. What about the others? The old Alpha had a son, right? A son who has mysteriously run off somewhere?"

"Uh, yeah." Reid shifted in his seat. "He had two of 'em, actually. I've only met the younger one, though. Kit Thornwood."

"What's he like?" I pressed.

"He's cool."

Ugh. I would get so much more out of Allara.

The clan was secretive, and the younger son of the old Alpha was cool. I couldn't tell if Reid was holding back on me for some reason, or if he genuinely didn't have any other information to share.

I might not have traveled far in my life, but I was still a shifter, and my shifter senses were on high alert. The farther we drove from the village, the edgier I became. The wolf in me was wary as all hell. Every bump in the road made me flinch in my seat.

If I'm heading into an unknown, I'd rather go in with my eyes open.

But I didn't bother trying to pry any further. For whatever reason, Reid clearly had no more information to provide. I would just have to wait and find out for myself when I arrived.

CHAPTER 2

KARA

It was mid-morning by the time the truck rolled to a stop at the edge of the Thornwood settlement. The perimeter was surrounded by a high wall and, as we approached the gates, a couple of figures stationed in a watchtower turned around to look at us, then disappeared from view.

A guarded perimeter, with watchtowers? *That's not creepy at all.*

The gates slowly started to open. Reid tapped the steering wheel a couple of times, then drove forward, toward the small group of shifters clustered around the entrance. He brought the truck to a standstill and glanced at me as he put his hand on the door.

"Wait here, yeah?"

"Sure." I nodded and watched as he climbed out of the car, my heart pounding in my chest. I was perfectly happy for him to take the lead at this point. I had never done anything like this before—visiting as the representative of our Alpha. I hardly even knew how I was supposed to behave.

I sat bolt upright in the passenger seat as a group of shifters approached Reid. They looked like a welcoming party, of sorts, though the expression on their faces was not what I'd call friendly.

Reid reached the group and clasped hands with a couple of the men, exchanging a few words with them. I tried to read their lips, but they were too far away.

Reid's posture was loose and easy. I allowed myself to relax a fraction, taking a deep, calming breath. I would take my cue from him.

They're our allies. They're not gonna hurt us—not without good reason, anyway.

Most of the men in the group peeled away after they'd spoken to Reid, and wandered out of sight. One of them remained. He continued to speak with Reid, his hands waving in the air in an expressive way that looked more human than shifter.

Reid nodded at whatever he was saying, so I took the opportunity to study the other man. His hair was lighter than most of the shifters I knew. Burnished strands caught the light, flashing auburn when he moved into a patch of sunlight shining through the trees. He had a soft, easy smile, and even from this distance, that smile made me want to smile, too.

He clapped Reid on the back before turning away and loping off in the same direction as the others.

Reid jogged back to the truck and slid behind the wheel. He seemed happy enough. "Let's park, and then I'll introduce you to everyone."

Another twinge of nerves shot through my chest as my heart continued to pound like I was running a marathon. I had to let some of my nervous tension go, before I ruined this for Allara.

"Sounds good." I forced a smile as he swung the truck around, and we trundled over to a small patch of grass where several other vehicles were parked.

This time, I was first out of the truck. I pushed the door open as soon as Reid turned off the engine, anxious to stretch and move. The second my feet touched the grass, my wolf wanted to bolt off into the forest.

Don't be stupid. There's nothing to be afraid of. Don't screw this up!

I swallowed the thickness in my throat. Reid came around to my side of the vehicle. He grinned down at me, and I wondered whether he was oblivious to the anxiety thrumming in my chest, or simply ignoring it in the hope I would get myself under control. Knowing Reid, and his heightened senses, it was probably the latter.

"You ready?" he asked.

My stomach churned. Still, I nodded.

"C'mon. Their meeting house is this way."

I followed Reid across a clearing toward a collection of small homes. Other than that first group of men who had assembled to greet Reid, I hadn't seen more than one or two others. Where was everyone? A couple of people passed us as we made our way down what I took to be the main street, but I caught movement at some of the windows. One of the chimneys was belching smoke.

My shifter senses told me that we were being watched and it made the hairs on the back of my neck stand on end. I hadn't expected anything else of course, but it was creepy being here, knowing that there were eyes on us, but not being able to see exactly where they were.

Like us, these people probably weren't used to outsiders, and given the fence and the watchtowers, they seemed even more guarded in this community than our own.

I recognized the meeting house. It was the biggest building in sight, for one thing. Unlike ours, it had a second floor, and the wide porch area underneath the jutting balcony was crowded with what looked like most of the Thornwood pack.

Okay, so that's where everyone is hiding. No wonder the village seems so empty. Looks like all the action is here.

Several heads turned as we approached, eyeing us as we climbed the stairs to the main doors. A couple of women had auburn hair similar to the guy Reid had spoken to. Theirs was brighter, like copper, and braided back into an intricate fishtail pattern.

As we headed inside, everyone moved back, leaving a wide berth around us, before following us inside, albeit at a distance.

I couldn't shake the worry that we were surrounded by people who could turn on us in a heartbeat.

Inside, the meeting house was already half-full of pack members. They were clustered in small groups on several rows of low benches that faced an empty stage, like they were waiting for something to begin.

We were halfway down the central aisle when a man sidled in front of us, blocking us from going any further. I tensed up. Reid put a warning hand on my arm, and I forced myself to relax somewhat, at least on the outside. Nothing I could about the inner nerves, except keep them hidden.

The man held up his hands, catching my expression. "Whoa! Didn't mean to startle you there, missy."

I took a closer look at him. He had a broad, open face, and his hair had that same deep auburn color as many of the others, but his was streaked with gray at the temples, as was his beard.

"Elder Frey." Reid identified the speaker before moving forward, his voice warm as he clasped the other man's hand and forearm. "It's good to see you again."

"And you, my boy." The Elder looked Reid up and down. "Not much of a boy these days, I see! You've grown into a fine man."

Reid chuckled. "Left boyhood behind a while back. It's been a long time, huh?"

"Too long." Elder Frey clapped a hand on one of Reid's shoulders. "I hear congratulations are in order. Allara's expecting, I take it?"

Reid's expression warmed, and his eyes lit up. "Yes. It won't be long now."

"Wonderful news." After another thud of approval on Reid's shoulder, Elder Frey stepped back. "Well, hopefully we can get this business over and done with so you can return to your family."

"That's the plan."

The Elder's gaze traveled over Reid's shoulder and landed on me. "And you must be Kara."

"Yes." I found my voice, glad it didn't come out on a squeak, and raised my chin before extending a hand for him to shake. "I'm—I'm here on our Alpha's behalf."

Elder Frey nodded. "Yes, Allara sent word. Very well. Follow me, you two. Let's go somewhere quiet where we can talk properly."

Reid and I followed the Elder to the back of the room, then through a small door that led up a narrow flight of stairs and into an upper room. Thick, wooden beams supported the high ceiling, and the desk in front of the window was overflowing with papers.

The guy Reid had spoken to earlier—the one with the contagious grin—stood in the middle of the room. He raised a hand in greeting, throwing us a lopsided smile.

Up close, I realized that he was young—in his late teens, by the look of it. His limbs had a coltish, awkward look to them, like he hadn't grown into his frame yet. But I'd been right about his manner. He gave the impression of friendliness rather than hostility, and I relaxed more in his presence.

"Hey." He came bounding up to us. "Kara, right?" He reminded me of Jason, back when we were still growing up and didn't have a care in the world. He shook my hand enthusiastically and I forgot, for just a second, to be afraid at all.

"Yes." I grinned back at him, charmed already.

"Kara," Reid interjected. "This is Kit Thornwood."

The Alpha's youngest son? "Nice to meet you," I said.

So this is the 'cool' younger brother. Where's his older brother, then? The supposed next Alpha?

The rest of the room was empty. There was nowhere for anyone else to hide. And besides, hadn't the other brother run off? He was probably out there lurking in the woods somewhere.

I glanced at Reid, but he wasn't looking in my direction. Instead, he was studying Kit and the Elder.

"Take a seat," Elder Frey said as he sank into a well-worn armchair.

Reid and I sat on the couch opposite it. Kit dragged over the desk chair and sat in it, crossing his ankles and swiveling back and forth in an annoying manner.

"Kit..." The Elder put a foot on the edge of the chair and brought it to a halt. "Stop that."

Kit bit his lip. His eyes darted toward the door, like he expected it to open, but no-one else entered the room.

"Fine." He spread out his hands and turned to Reid. "Where do you wanna begin? Do you want to go first, or shall I?"

Elder Frey coughed, but Reid didn't seem bothered by the informality. If anything, he looked more relaxed by the way this meeting was being handled.

As did I. If this was a pack business meeting, with an Alpha's son swinging on a chair, then surely, I could handle this, too?

I reminded myself that stuffy bureaucracy was never Reid's thing, either. *The guy didn't want to wear a suit to his own wedding, for crying out loud.*

"How about I start?" Reid said.

Kit shrugged. "Works for me."

"Great." Reid's deep voice filled the room. He'd settled into the leadership role with ease, even here, on another pack's land. He was the kind of person who naturally drew a crowd. A born leader, alongside his mate. "As you know, we had some trouble a few months back with one of our pack members, Jaime."

Kit nodded, exchanging glances with Elder Frey before waiting for Reid to continue.

"Jaime was like a son to Allara's dad. After she left, everyone assumed he'd take over as Alpha." Reid paused, his jaw tightening. "When the old Alpha died, he named his daughter as his successor."

I thought back to the day Allara had returned to the village. The five years she'd been gone had melted away almost immediately. She came back almost the same brash, outspoken girl I'd grown up with. Only there were subtle differences, too. Her experiences in the city had matured her into a formidable woman. An Alpha, through and through. We were lucky to have her as our Alpha.

"Allara claimed the position of Alpha by defeating Jaime in combat." A shadow fell over Reid's face. "But she chose not to kill him. Jaime's still out there. That's the reason we're here. Allara wants to strengthen the alliance between the Thornwoods and the Banes before Jaime has the chance to spread his poison any further."

Silence fell over the room. Reid leaned forward, addressing Elder Frey directly. "Tell me, has Jaime made contact with you in any way?"

The Elder shook his head. "No. We keep our borders secure, as you saw on your way in. There's no way he could breach our defenses. Not without us knowing about it."

Don't be so sure about that. You don't know him like we do.

I'd known Jaime my whole life. Like all shifters, he didn't give up easy, and he had a cunning streak a mile wide. Sometimes I used to think he was more snake than wolf.

Reid seemed satisfied, however, as he leaned back against the sofa and turned his attention to Kit. "Why don't you give me an update on your news. What's been going on here that's got everyone so riled up?"

We both knew, of course, about the Thornwood Alpha's death. It was the event that had caused the power vacuum, but it was obvious there was more to the story.

I spoke up then, knowing it would be something Allara wanted said upfront. "Our pack sends its condolences on your father's passing, Kit."

Reid shot me a look laced with approval.

"Thank you." Kit's bright features dimmed a little as he recounted his father's death. I caught a glimpse of the sadness underlying his cheerful personality.

"So, my brother was considering accepting the position of Alpha, and things were all set for him to take over." Kit started jiggling his knee up and down again, but catching a look from Elder Frey, he stopped. "Then on the day of the ceremony, he just... took off. Shifted and disappeared into the forest before anyone could do anything to stop him, or ask what was going on. Nobody's seen him since."

Reid and I exchanged a glance.

"Did he say anything before he left?" I asked.

Kit shook his head. "Nothing. I don't know what happened... and neither does anyone else. But now we don't have an Alpha, and everything's screwed up."

So, it was as bad as Allara had suspected. Not only did the Thornwoods not have an Alpha, but the one who should rightfully inherit the role was AWOL, and the next in line was just a kid.

Kit seemed like a delightful person, but he didn't strike me as someone strong enough to lead a pack. From the look on Reid's face, he shared my thoughts on that, but when he spoke, his tone remained even and calm. He was doing a good job of masking any concern he might be feeling. "Do you know where he might be? Can we assist in searching for him?"

Kit hung his head. "Nah. The truth is, I don't think he wants to be found. And when my brother wants to disappear, it's pointless trying to look for him. He's likely long gone by now."

My heart thumped in my chest. The small office suddenly felt too cluttered, too hot and stuffy.

I stood up and crossed over to the window, cracking it open and inhaling a lungful of fresh air. It was clear and crisp outside, and the deserted village scene served to calm my senses. It would be a while before I adjusted to all the new smells and sounds that this place had to offer, but I wasn't getting any impression of threat. On the contrary, with Elder Frey and Kit temporarily in charge, I felt like we were with allies.

Then my body tensed as something strange prickled at my senses. My attention was drawn to a flicker of movement. It was coming from the edge of the square. The same direction Reid and I had come in from.

My skin crawled with alarm when a huge wolf loped into the clearing. Its long, reddish-brown fur was matted and its paws dirt-crusted. Even from this distance, I could see leaves and mud in its fur. But its movement was confident and sure.

The wolf didn't seem hurt. On the contrary, it was walking like it owned the place. Its head was high, and its strides were long, as if it were familiar with this place and knew exactly where it was headed.

Once the wolf reached the middle of the square, it stopped and gave a full-bodied shake, dislodging most of the leaves and muck. By the look of what fell off it, the beast had dragged half the forest into town on its back.

The wolf lowered its huge head, and the air grew hazy with the tell-tale sign that a shifter was transforming. Once the haze cleared, a man stood in place of the wolf.

He was one of the tallest and most impressively muscled men I'd ever seen. Like Kit, he had burnished auburn hair, although his was longer and darker, partly obscuring his face. His body was strong and well-built. A heated flush rose in my cheeks at his brazenness. The way he stood naked outside the meeting house, totally at ease with his body, did something to my insides.

He shook the hair out of his eyes and looked up. His gaze locked straight onto mine.

The breath left my body when our eyes met. I bit my lip, embarrassed to have been caught spying, but for some reason I couldn't look away. He held my attention like he had every right to it.

Suddenly, I was the one who felt naked.

I'd been so caught up in the arrival of this stranger, I hadn't noticed that the others in the room had moved to the window and were all standing next to me, gazing down at the guy in the town square.

"Who..." My voice sounded husky. I cleared my throat and didn't finish.

It was Kit who eventually answered my unspoken question. "That's Ronan." He said it slowly, like he couldn't believe his eyes. "That's my missing brother."

CHAPTER 3

RONAN

I knew I had to return to town as soon as I saw the truck approach the gates. Elder Frey was too old, and Kit was far too young, to face down any potential threat on their own. I needed to be there to protect them, and not just by keeping watch within the tree line.

From my vantage position in the forest, I was perfectly positioned to watch everyone who came and went, and I had been keeping a close eye on all movement in and out of my pack's village. I knew every vehicle by sight; every dirt bike, every rust-bucket on wheels that my packmates drove.

This truck, carrying strangers, made my internal alarm go berserk.

As they had approached the perimeter wall I padded through the trees, my belly low to the earth. It was easy to track the rumble of their engine along the straight road, and I ducked back into the undergrowth every time I felt too exposed.

I got the sense that they didn't know I was there, following their truck right up to the gate.

I wasn't close enough to see who the visitors were, but something in my stomach twisted with unease. Was this the threat that sought to tear my pack apart?

My hackles rose as the gate opened and the visitors were allowed to pass through without incident. My lips peeled back in a silent growl when a tall man jumped down from the driver's side, striding forward like he owned the place.

That one was an Alpha, for sure.

At the sight of my little brother jogging forward to greet him, I couldn't help the snarl that rumbled through me. My muscles coiled, preparing to spring...

The man got back in his truck and the high gates closed behind them, cutting off my view of what was happening inside the village.

Strange, being on the outside of my own pack like this.

My exile might have been self-imposed, but it wasn't without good reason. No matter who I'd hurt by my decision—my brother, my friends, Jake and Noah, and even Elder Frey—I knew eventually they would understand.

I hadn't left them unprotected, as they all likely thought. I hadn't run off, due to cowardice. Was it time to come forward, out of hiding at last?

I brushed the leaves aside and trotted out into the open, ducking my head to examine the track marks in the dirt.

I sniffed at the air and a barrage of different sensations hit me.

With a deep huff, I forced myself to separate them out, so I could identify them, one by one.

The truck contained only two individuals, by my reckoning. Both shifters, one male and one female.

Mates?

No, they weren't a bonded pair. They were definitely from the same clan, though—and I knew the scent. I'd picked it up from somewhere before.

But which clan? Silverback? Ferrers?

I inhaled again, more deeply this time. *Bane.*

Though unsettling to scent a neighboring pack member or two on our land, it wasn't the smell of the Bane pack that had me on such high alert.

It was the female. I had never smelled anything like her before; she had a sweet, light scent that made my mouth water and my system switch into hyper-alert mode. It was like finding a clear, bubbling stream after crawling through the desert for years.

I wanted to throw back my head and howl into the sky.

With effort, I restrained myself.

I loped back into the trees, horrified at the urges I could barely control. After weeks of carefully evading the attention of the pack, I'd almost blown my cover over some random chick.

Don't think about that. Come on, focus. Why do you know that scent? You've never visited the Bane Clan.

Maybe not, but some of their members had come around these parts in the past. I must have picked the scent up from Kit. He'd run into them once, several years back.

He was always the more sociable one of us.

Fate had some sense of humor, making me the firstborn.

I circled the edge of the village a few times, sticking close to the walls of the perimeter. There was no sign of life from either the forest or the watchtowers that were stationed around the outside of town. Everyone must have gathered in the meeting house.

Trying to decide what to do in my absence, undoubtedly.

A stab of guilt shot through me. It was no use. I couldn't stay away from my destiny. I was the Alpha's firstborn, for better or worse, and I had to go back. I'd always known I would. Otherwise, I would have been halfway to Canada by now.

Instead, I'd stayed close, watchful and aware, in case my pack needed me. And now they did.

I had to set things right, or at least be held accountable for my actions.

With a deep sigh, I turned around, heading back toward the front gates.

~

KARA

I tried to speak, but it was no use. My muscles were all locked up, and the air had deserted my lungs. *What the heck is wrong with me?*

Luckily, Reid broke the silence for all of us.

"Wait, *that's* Ronan Thornwood? The next Alpha of the Thornwood Clan?"

It was clear, judging by the tone of his voice, that he was in just as much shock as I was. However, he didn't seem to have experienced the same intense, dizzying bolt of electricity as me at the very sight of the auburn-haired shifter.

On the contrary, Reid was frowning through the window at the figure making his way up the steps of the meeting house, and he looked confused rather than impressed.

"Where the hell's he been all this time?" Reid's tone was laced with bewilderment.

Kit shrugged, pure joy written across his features. He clearly didn't care whether his brother had been. He was focused only on the face that Ronan had returned. Kit bounded over to the door.

"Come on!" he called, before vanishing through the doorway.

Reid and I glanced back at Elder Frey, who merely threw up his hands in an *I-have-no-idea* kind of way and slumped down on the sofa with a weary expression.

Reid and I headed down the narrow wooden staircase, more

slowly than Kit. When we reached the bottom, Kit didn't head into the main room, where the majority of the pack were still waiting for the meeting to start, but slipped out the front door and onto the porch.

Reid looked at me, shrugged, and followed after him.

After a split-second hesitation, with my heart thumping a mile a minute in my chest, I headed through the door, too.

Ronan, the next Alpha of the Thornwood pack, waited for us on the porch.

The air around him had a sharp, earthy smell, like it was going to rain.

I was suddenly aware of every little detail of my surroundings. The uneven floorboards beneath my feet, the weathered siding on the wall, and even the uneven rasping of my own breath in my ears as I came face to face with Ronan.

He was barefoot. Mercifully, he'd pulled on a pair of beat-up looking jeans from God-knows-where. I'm not sure what I would have done if he was still fully naked. Judging by my skittishness, quite possibly turned tail and scurried straight back up to sit on the sofa with Elder Frey. His chest was still bare, though, and he was breathing heavily from the aftermath of shifting. A fine sheen of sweat coated his skin, highlighting the defined muscle and sinew of his arms.

Damn, he's gorgeous.

His eyes slid from Kit to Reid and then me, and his expression darkened, like clouds drifting to cover the sun. "Who are you?"

His voice was dark and rough, and rippled over me in a strange yet compelling manner. When he spoke, all the hairs on the back of my neck stood on end.

Reid seemed to be affected, too, which made me feel slightly less embarrassed at my reaction. I was used to Alpha's—I was the friend of Allara, for heaven's sake—but this one seemed to leave everyone around him breathless.

Reid visibly took one breath, and then another. It was a familiar

trick that shifters often used when they needed to ground themselves in an unfamiliar environment, or deal with someone their
inner shifter perceived as a rival.

Ronan had no such compunctions. I caught a flicker in his eyes.
His shifter was still close to the surface, waiting and watching.

"Reid, of the Bane clan." Reid held out his hand with a thin smile
that held little humor. His eyes never left Ronan's. "And this is Kara.
She's standing in for our Alpha—my mate Allara—who couldn't
make it here today."

A muscle in Ronan's jaw twitched. He grabbed Reid's forearm,
and they shook in the traditional shifter way.

Then Ronan jerked Reid closer, teeth bared. "And *what* are you
doing on my pack grounds?"

Reid's lips pulled back into an open snarl. My hands were on his
shoulders before I could think, tugging helplessly. He shook me off
easily. He wasn't rough—Reid was still in there, after all—but it was
clear his shifter was rearing up and angling to be in the driver's seat.

Opposite me, Kit murmured in Ronan's ear, obviously taking the
same conciliatory role as me. Ronan's eyes flashed as he continued to
square up with Reid, but slowly, he began to back down from his
aggressive stance.

Reid stepped back as well. He glanced at me, giving a small nod
as if to confirm he had himself under control.

"We were hoping to rekindle our alliance with the Thornwood
pack," he said, stone-faced. "We had a situation a couple of months
back. One of our young males went rogue. He almost killed my
mate."

Reid stared at the ground, taking a further moment to calm
himself. His eyes were dark when he looked up again. "Allara and I
hoped we might be able to come to an understanding that would
benefit both packs."

Ronan tilted up his chin. The glint in his eyes told me he was
listening closely. Despite only being clad in the old jeans, he looked
every inch a leader.

"I see." He glanced toward the door. Through the glass panel to the side, several pack members watched the drama unfolding out on the porch.

They whispered back and forth to each other, and I couldn't tell if their interest lay with me and Reid, or if it was Ronan's sudden reappearance that had captured their attention.

"Why don't we continue this conversation inside?" I realized that Elder Frey stood in the doorway of the meeting house. He stepped out and put a hand on Kit's shoulder, steering him toward the front entrance. "Good to see you, Ronan. I'm sure the rest of the pack deserve to hear whatever this is about. In the interest of transparency, of course."

There was a note in his voice that spoke of annoyance. Was he annoyed with Reid and me, or Ronan? I couldn't tell, but Reid and I followed the Elder and Kit inside. Ronan moved fast, stepping past me to hold the door open for me and as I passed him, I was once again forced to inhale that intoxicating scent.

To my surprise, we didn't head to the long benches, where the rest of the pack were gathered. Instead, the Elder led us all the way down the aisle, toward the raised platform at the end of the room. At first I almost veered off, to sit to one side, but then I remembered.

Right. I'm meant to be standing in for Allara.

It was strange, playacting the role of Alpha. I felt like I was wearing someone else's clothes, and everyone could see how ill-fitting they really were. Like a child playacting at being an adult.

When we reached the foot of the platform, Ronan murmured to me, "Watch your step."

His gruff voice sent a shiver down my spine.

I wanted to roll my eyes, but I wasn't sure if it was at his words, or my physical reaction to his closeness.

I know how to walk up a few steps, thanks, was on the tip of my tongue, but in the end I bit my tongue. The stairs were a little uneven, and as I started to climb up to the stage, I faltered.

Ronan grabbed my hand to steady me. As soon as his fingers closed around mine, every nerve in my body lit up.

The sensation was instant and intense, like an electric current passing under my skin, flowing through his hand into mine. Our eyes locked, and my own shock was reflected back at me in his astonished gaze.

What the...?

For what felt like years, we stood there, connected by a single point. My hand in his. Nothing else mattered: the rest of the pack, even Reid. Everything faded into the background, except for the touch of Ronan's fingers that convulsed on my skin.

Abruptly, he dropped my hand and the moment dissipated. We climbed up onto the stage, but I couldn't forget. What just happened?

I glanced at Reid, who stared at me with a mild frown. *You okay?* he mouthed.

I nodded. It was only half a lie. I was okay and yet, somehow I wasn't. Something had changed deep inside me.

The eyes of the crowd passed over me and then Reid with mild curiosity. They seemed to be more focused on Ronan, who I didn't dare look at after that moment. I still felt his touch tingling all the way up my arm and down my left side. I was itching to touch him again, but managed to refrain, clenching them into fists by my side.

Whatever the hell just happened, it must have taken mere seconds.

Remember, you're here for Allara. You have to make a good impression. Don't blow this for her—or your pack.

I let myself be ushered by Elder Frey into one of the high-backed wooden chairs, the kind that council members usually sat in when our own meeting house was in session. I shifted in the seat, hot and uncomfortable, feeling the need to shift and head out for a run. I swallowed a couple of times, dry-mouthed.

Ronan's voice crept over me. I didn't know how he was just standing there, talking to his people like nothing had happened.

Maybe he hadn't felt... whatever it was. Maybe it was just me whose world had suddenly shifted on its axis?

"Our visitors from the Bane Clan have come to strengthen the bonds between our two packs."

The crowd murmured, and a few pairs of eyes flicked over to Reid and me with a little more interest this time.

"I want everyone to show them a warm welcome. I know I have some explaining to do regarding my recent absence." Ronan paused. The silence was deafening. "The explanation will come in due course, but for now, I'm afraid you will have to wait. In the meantime, I can assure you, I'm back now. For good."

"Does this mean the Alpha ceremony is back on?" someone from the back called out.

Several people clapped in agreement, until Ronan held up his hands and a hush fell once more.

Damn. He may not be the official pack Alpha yet, but his presence is compelling. These people certainly respect him.

"The truth is, both our packs are in danger—the Thornwoods, and the Banes. There are those out there who want to tear us apart, and not just from the outside. I want to stop that before it can take root. So, Reid and Kara will be staying with us indefinitely as ambassadors on behalf of their people," Ronan continued, ignoring the way Reid's head jerked sharply in surprise. "I hope their visit will bring our clans closer."

The murmuring grew louder. Eventually, scattered applause broke out.

Oh... crap. Were we prisoners of the Thornwood pack now?

Once it became clear that the show was over, the pack members began to get up from their seats and file out. The whole time I just sat there, frozen.

Once we were alone, Reid stood. All pretense at civility was forgotten as he rounded on Ronan with renewed aggravation.

"That's a kind invitation," he growled. "You could've told us you wanted us to stay before you announced it to your *entire* clan. And didn't give us a chance to refuse without looking boorish."

Ronan shrugged. At first glance, his posture was loose and easy, but the slight tension in his shoulders told another story.

"Look, if I'm going to agree to this alliance, I want to know who I'm getting into bed with. We only met a few minutes ago. I need more time." His eyes skimmed over mine. I couldn't stop the heated flush running up my neck. "Besides, it's a win-win. This way, we both get what we want—right?"

"My wife is giving birth in a matter of *days,*" Reid hissed. "There is no way I'm staying here. I will *not* miss the birth of my child."

"Fine." Ronan's voice was like steel. "Then you can leave. We'll take the girl."

"*What?*" Reid spluttered. "*No!*"

"The way I see it, your Alpha should've killed the one that betrayed your clan while she had the chance. You've brought this danger on all of us." Ignoring Reid's thunderous expression, Ronan's eyes wandered over to his brother and Elder Frey. "I'll keep my word, but I need to know that you'll keep yours. My pack is everything to me."

"Kara isn't a bargaining chip," Reid said firmly. "She's coming home with me, and that's that."

The two men stared at each other. Reid was clearly frustrated, but Ronan seemed impassive, like he couldn't care less one way or the other.

I don't buy that attitude for a second.

Time to do what Allara sent me here to do. I took a deep breath, and released it slowly. Finally, I spoke up. "I'll do it."

CHAPTER 4

KARA

The loudness of my voice startled me.

Everyone turned in my direction. Kit and Elder Frey seemed mildly surprised, and Reid's eyebrows drew down. But it was Ronan whose expression intrigued me the most.

His eyes pierced mine as he gazed down at me. Most of the shifters I knew had eyes that ranged from warm, chocolate brown to light hazel, the color of sunlight shining through spring leaves.

Ronan's, however, were a sharp, unyielding amber. Every detail of his features overwhelmed me. The line of his jaw, his rumpled hair.

Not to mention the fact he's still half-naked. Can we postpone this thing and find the guy a shirt already?

"Kara." Reid's voice drifted in from the sidelines. "You don't have to—"

My head jerked to catch his eye. "I know. But I *want* to."

I tried to communicate everything I couldn't say out loud in a look. I knew that we didn't have much time left, and I wanted him to tell Allara I would be okay.

This is the right thing to do. If I can get these people to trust me, we have a real shot at standing our ground against Jaime, if and when he does decide he wants to make a move.

Reid blinked. Something in my face must have communicated what I was thinking, because he gave a short nod and stepped back.

With the other three men, Elder Frey, Kit and Reid, standing behind us in a loose half circle, Ronan and I were face to face.

My skin prickled uncomfortably. Something about the setting—the fact we were still in the meeting house—made this feel like more than a political agreement.

It feels like a bonding ceremony.

I shoved the thought out of my mind just as Ronan held out his arm.

Taking a deep breath, like I was about to plunge into an icy pool, I gripped his forearm, just beneath the elbow. He did the same to mine.

Sensation flooded through me. It was exactly like our encounter on the steps, except...

Stronger. Much stronger.

I couldn't let go of him. I didn't *want* to let go. I was trapped like a fly in those amber eyes, and I would happily drown if it meant he would continue touching my skin. Frenzied thoughts raced through my mind, my imagination spiraling beyond control.

If a simple handshake feels this good...

I went weak at the knees. For a split second, I was terrified I'd literally melt into the floor, but I managed to stand my ground.

And yet...

There's something else. Something that wasn't there before.

I couldn't chase the thought to its conclusion. In the heat of the moment, I couldn't bring myself to care. I just needed more—needed him to pull me close so that I could feel the heat of his skin through my clothes.

It was only when I wrenched my hand away in a panic, gasping, that I realized *what*, exactly, was different.

This time, we weren't alone.

This time, everyone else had noticed it, too.

RONAN

"The two of you are fated mates," Reid declared in a shocked tone, the words booming around me like a cannon.

The hall was empty now. The rest of the pack had returned to their usual duties after I dismissed them from the meeting. Only the five of us remained. The Elder, my brother and I, along with our visitors.

The Alpha male of the Bane Clan, Reid, rambled on, but I was only half paying attention to the explanation.

I heard the words *bonded* and *ideal partner* in a strange, muted way. Like I was deep underwater, and the words were floating down to me from the surface. With each passing moment, my heart beat faster and faster, like it was searching for a way out of my chest and would explode if I didn't let it out.

Eventually I'd had enough. I looked up, my jaw so tight I could barely force the words out.

"All right. I understand." When Elder Frey frowned I realized my tone was too rough. I growled out a belated, "thank you," in the direction of Reid.

I couldn't even look at the girl.

Kara. My brain seemed determined to acknowledge her, even though my heart did not want it. *Her name is Kara.*

She wasn't the type of woman I usually gravitated to. Not that I'd dated anyone seriously, but my brief flings of the past had all tended toward the blonde, bubbly variety. Human women, for the most part. I liked that they knew nothing about me, nothing of who I was. They had no expectations, beyond wanting a bit of fun. Which suited me just fine.

This girl was a dark brunette. Her blue eyes were so pale they verged on gray. With her pointed chin and dainty, slender frame, it was difficult to see the shifter in her at all. She certainly didn't look like she knew how to party. She looked like she'd never even heard the word, fun.

I'd never given much thought to finding a mate.

And even if I had...

This petite, quiet creature? Really? Where's the fierce she-wolf they say all Alpha women must be?

In all the stories my mother had read to me growing up, fated mates were like two halves of one soul. They hunted together, fought off rivals, raised their young, and basically did everything that made up a shifter's life, together. Most Alpha wolves in the old tales were fierce warriors, and their women were more than a match for their strength in battle.

I'd always assumed that if I ever found a mate, she would match my passion in bed, also.

This one—Kara—looked like she'd snap in two if I tried anything close to passionate with her.

"It's literally *fate* that you came here!" Kit piped up, throwing a sunny smile in Kara's direction. Despite my misgivings, my heart warmed at my brother's optimism. He was always the one of us to see the best in people.

Kara smiled back at him. "It seems so."

I had to admit, standing here with her beside me was becoming increasingly uncomfortable. When she thought I wasn't looking, her eyes kept dancing over my torso in a way that made me think she'd prefer it if I wasn't wearing any pants.

The wolf in me wanted to gather her into my arms and head off into the woods, far from prying eyes. The *man* in me, luckily, knew that that was an insane idea.

You don't even know this girl, and now you want to kidnap her? You're losing it, Ronan.

"When will you head home, Reid?" Elder Frey got to his feet, addressing the male guest.

"I'm not sure. Tomorrow at the latest, given Allara's condition..." Reid stopped, his gaze sliding to Kara. He clearly felt guilty about even thinking of leaving her here alone. In fact, he looked downright pissed at the idea.

She gave him a quick smile. "I'll be fine."

Elder Frey cleared his throat. "Maybe you and Kit would like to show our guests around the village, Ronan." He turned to Kit and me with a smile. "I would join you, but I'm afraid I have some matters to attend to."

"Yes. All right," I said. Anything to break the strange tension encapsulating us.

The four of us headed out into the town square. Reid was frowning again, not at anything in particular. He still seemed displeased by the revelation that Kara and I were connected in some way.

When Kara caught hold of his arm, a jolt of jealousy mixed with a twinge of anxiety shivered through me.

Has she changed her mind already, so soon?

The thought of her leaving was suddenly impossible to contemplate. I blinked, trying to rein in my errant and irrational feelings.

"You should go now." Kara looked up at Reid. Her face was full of warm understanding. "I'll be all right, Reid. It's time for you to return to your wife."

Reid looked down at her. His eyes darted from me, to Kit, back down to Kara, then off to the side, downcast. "I... I can't just..."

"Yes," Kara said, more firmly this time. She squeezed his arm to draw his attention back to her. "You can. You said it yourself, Allara's due any day now. There's no way you're missing the birth of your first child because of me. Allara would never forgive me!"

"C'mon, Kara—"

"I don't need babysitting." Kara tilted her head, affection and exasperation coloring her voice. "I'm a grownup, Reid. I can take care of myself, all right?"

"I know that," Reid grumbled. "Are you sure?"

"Absolutely." Kara gave him a smile that didn't quite reach her eyes, but Reid didn't seem to notice the underlying tension in his pack mate.

I noticed. I wanted to fold her into my arms and tell her she really would be okay. I scowled at the direction of my thoughts.

Reid frowned down at her, then pulled her into a bear hug, his biceps tight around her slender shoulders.

There it was again, unmistakable this time. *Jealousy.* Like acid eating at my gut from the inside.

I wanted to drag him off her, and settle this in a fight. Our shifters would resolve it soon enough. It was a crazy thought, but it was there, nonetheless.

When they pulled back from each other, he ruffled her hair like she was his kid sister, and she shoved his hands away from her. They both laughed.

All the amusement drained from Reid's face as he stepped in close to me. A muscle twitched in his jaw, and his hands flexed by his sides, like he was itching to throw a punch.

He clearly cared for her, which was the only reason I kept my shifter reined in tightly against his aggressive stance.

"If you hurt her," he said in a low, deadly voice, "I'll end you. Got it?"

I met his eyes. The shifter in me wanted to fight back, to challenge him right there and then, but my survival instincts told me to hold back.

"Got it," I said in a carefully neutral tone.

Besides, I kind of respected the guy. I liked the fact that Kara had someone who'd protected her up until now. And I wasn't going to hurt her. Not unless she liked it rough in bed, and then I could get as creative as she wanted.

Apparently satisfied, Reid stepped back. Kara was wide-eyed. Her gaze darted between the two of us, like she was expecting a full-on fight to break out at any moment.

Kit broke the silence, sidling up to Reid.

"Come on." He shoved his hands in his pockets and nodded in the direction of the road leading out of town. "I'll walk you back to your truck."

With one final stony look at me, and a parting, anxious stare for Kara, Reid allowed himself to be led away.

Which left the two of us—me and Kara—alone.

For the very first time, my brain pointed out helpfully. *Let's try not to screw this up, Thornwood.*

I could barely look her in the eye. Which was ridiculous; especially if we were destined for each other. And every instinct was telling me we were.

Yet we were still total strangers.

Where were the rose petals and violins, the tearful vows of eternal devotion? All that crap was nowhere to be found. This was worse than an awkward first date.

"Come on," I muttered, before the silence stretched out even longer. "I'll give you the grand tour."

Kara

I was doing my best to concentrate as Ronan led me down the main street, but my head buzzed wildly.

What the hell are you doing? You're smack in the middle of a rival pack, totally alone. No protection except my wits and whatever strength

43

my shifter wolf gave me.

What made you think this was a good idea?

Of course, the answer lay ahead of me in the form of Ronan, the muscles of his back flexing as he strode onwards ahead of me. He occasionally glanced back to make sure I was keeping up with him, but he made no real concession for my shorter legs in his stride.

Every time our eyes met, the rush of electricity was almost overwhelming—and definitely like nothing I'd ever felt before today.

The truth was, I'd never even been with a man—*any* man, much less one who ignited such a strong spark of desire in my belly. There hadn't been much opportunity back at our village; my options were kind of limited. There was Reid, who had always been Allara's and who I saw as a brother more than anything else, and Jaime and his gang. They were my brother's friends, which was kind of a turn-off.

Who was I kidding? It wasn't like no-one had offered. I knew several men in our clan who would have happily taken me for a mate if I'd shown them any interest whatsoever.

I'd just never felt that *spark.* Damn spark.

It was stupid, but on some level, I'd always craved what Reid and Allara had, but had come to the conclusion a while back that it likely wasn't going to happen for me.

I'd grown up with Allara and Reid, after all. I'd had a lifetime of knowing what a true bond was supposed to look like. A perfect relationship with someone who was my ideal match.

I knew it was naïve. Even with Reid and Allara, it hadn't been smooth sailing, but I couldn't help the way I felt.

Now, it looks like I've got my wish. And I'm not sure how I feel about it.

Ronan Thornwood was nothing like my idea of an Alpha. All the Alphas I'd known—Allara and her father, even Reid—were all warm, gentle, and extroverted. Tough when they needed to be, but always quick to pull anyone who looked like they needed it into a hug.

It was difficult to imagine this man acting that way.

I was so caught up in my thoughts that I didn't realize Ronan had come to a halt outside a wooden dwelling until I almost crashed into his muscled back.

The dwelling was a simple A-frame structure, bigger than the ones farther down the street. A claw-print was carved into the cross-beam above the front door.

"This is the Alpha's house." Ronan swept a careless hand up at the façade of the building. "My brother and I live here."

I made some noise of acknowledgement that seemed to satisfy him, because we moved past the house and continued down the street.

The scant information he'd given me was intriguing. The way he'd said *the Alpha's house*, was strange. Like the house itself didn't belong to him and Kit. It sounded like they were just occupying it, for now.

A million questions crowded in the back of my mind, but I didn't have the nerve to voice them.

What was it like growing up here, with your parents? Does the house feel too big, too empty now that they're gone? Where did you run off to, and why? And why did you come back, today of all days?

We walked around the perimeter of the town, sticking close to the high fences that surrounded it. My stomach twisted. It all felt unnatural, existing so close to the forest, yet being cut off from it by a manmade structure.

Completely unlike our pack village, which was more in tune with its natural surrounds.

"This is the East watchtower." Ronan pointed up at a tall structure at the edge of the town.

A man inside spotted us and waved.

"You can see the forest for miles around up there."

"Impressive," I said. "But why?"

Ronan looked puzzled. "What do you mean?"

"No offence. It's just that this place is like a fortress."

Ronan smiled ruefully.

My heart sank. "I'm sorry. I haven't seen much outside my own village, you see, and ours doesn't look like... this."

"Don't apologize. I get how it must look to an outsider." Ronan stared up at the high wall, but his expression was distant, contemplative. "My father was a vigilant man, I guess you could say."

At my questioning look, he shrugged. "Some might call it paranoia. It got worse as he got older. He started to question old alliances and treaties. He had it in his head that the other clans were out to get us. He used to tell my brother and I that they wanted to steal our land and take our women, all that crap. So, he built these walls. In his mind, he was keeping us safe."

I couldn't stop the shiver that ran through me.

"Anyway." Ronan threw me a forced smile, as if slightly awkward about sharing anything personal. "Mom reined him in, when she was alive. They were... y'know..."

Fated mates, I finished in my head. *Got it.*

As we turned back toward the main road, I couldn't hold back the curiosity that itched inside my chest.

"Back there." I glanced up at him. It was getting easier to meet his eyes. "Why did you agree to let Reid go? I'm... I'm nobody, Ronan. I'm not an Alpha. I'm not Allara. We all know that. So, why me?"

"I didn't want Allara," Ronan said simply. "Or Reid."

I blinked. "Oh."

He turned away, leaving me to stare at his retreating back and ponder what the hell, exactly, he meant by *that*.

RONAN

It was nearing lunchtime by the time Kara and I made our way back to the village square. Several people were milling around; a couple of them looked like they might talk to me, so I skirted near to the edge of the clearing until I found my brother leaning against one of the posts outside the meeting house.

He brightened up when he saw me, offering a familiar, sunny smile. Something in my chest tightened. I'd missed him more than I realized.

"Hey!" Kit waved at us as we got within talking range. "I was about to head home and grab something to eat. You guys wanna come with me?"

I glanced down at Kara, who nodded. "Sure, I could eat."

"Awesome." Kit fell into step beside me as we walked toward the main track. "I was thinking mac 'n cheese!"

It was obvious how relieved Kit was to see me, but he kept the flow of conversation light and casual as we walked. I knew he wouldn't ask about what happened until I opened up and told him. Nobody knew me better than Kit, and he knew not to push until I was ready.

As I walked side-by-side with Kara, our arms occasionally brushed. Every time, it sent a spark of electricity through me. I clenched my teeth, forcing myself to focus on the discussion.

"So, is this place any different from what you're used to?" Kit asked Kara.

Kara shrugged, scuffing the edge of her shoe against the gravel path. Her eyes wandered over to the high fence.

"Some things. But the people seem nice." She gave Kit a friendly smile, clearly unwilling to criticize anything here in front of Kit. I appreciated her kindness. "You've all been very welcoming so far."

I thought back to the moment at the meeting house, to my insane decision to have her stay here in a flash of pure, unadulterated instinct. I was regretting it more and more with each passing moment.

Now I've trapped her here. This meek, shy girl who has hardly set foot outside her own village. Of all the people I could hold here as a bargaining chip, Kara is the least suitable for that role.

When we reached the Alpha's house, we climbed up the steps to our front door. Kara's eyes wandered over the bear claw carving. As Kit opened the door, I came to stand beside her.

"My grandfather's handiwork," I said. She looked up at me with those sweet blue eyes and it was an effort to turn my face away. "He carved it the day he and my grandmother were bonded together."

She stared up at the carving, a soft smile crossing over her features as she studied it. What was she thinking? Then she dropped her gaze, her eyes shuttered, as she entered through the doorway. I reached up and ran a hand over the carving before I followed her. I had never properly noticed it before today. It was just a part of life, as familiar as the sky, but the way she had looked at it—*really* looked—made me take more notice, too.

Kit and Kara had already gravitated into the kitchen. Kara stood to the side, her arms wrapped protectively around her middle. I pulled out a barstool and she hopped onto it, swinging her legs back and forth like a kid.

"I hope you don't take this the wrong way..." She bit her lip and stopped speaking.

I had to look away from the sight of those perfect white teeth sinking into reddened flesh. Internally, I groaned, my mind going to exactly where I wanted her to bite me.

"Your house is *way* tidier than I expected for two young guys living alone."

Kit smirked. He was pulling pots and pans out of the kitchen cupboards and laying them on the sideboard with swift, confident motions.

I wish I could be anywhere near that level of calm right now.

"Kit's the neat freak," I admitted as I pulled out the stool beside hers. Her cheeks reddened as she tucked a loose strand of hair behind her ear and laughed. "I can't take responsibility for any of this."

"Yeah, it's been way easier than usual keeping this place clean over the past couple of weeks." Kit averted his gaze from mine as he opened the fridge. It was the first time he'd brought up my disappearance, and there was a note in his voice that stung. I'd clearly hurt him, with my disappearance, but he was too kind to say that straight out.

By the time he turned, his arms full of ingredients, he was smiling again and it was as if he hadn't said anything untoward. "Hey, why don't you show Kara around while I cook? No offense, dude, but it'll be awkward having you two sitting here staring at me the whole time."

I raised an eyebrow. If my extroverted, cheerful brother was feeling awkward, then that was really saying something.

Not to mention, there's not much to see. It's just a house...

Kara was already on her feet. "Oh my God, can I do anything to help? I'm kind of a useless cook, but I can peel vegetables, or..."

"No!" Kit flapped a tea towel at her before she could get too close to the stove. "Seriously, I'm fine. Go with Ronan."

He shot a look at me that was followed by something dangerously close to a smirk.

Oh, God. Was my brother... *matchmaking*?

"Go have fun, okay?" Kit said, and Kara's face flushed even darker. As she scurried out of the kitchen, I glared daggers at my brother, who was struggling not to laugh.

You're welcome, he mouthed to me, with a wide grin.

In the hallway, Kara was waiting for me. She smiled as I approached, and I found myself smiling back. Something inside me wanted to open up to her, to show her how I truly felt. It was an unnerving sensation and one I was definitely not used to.

"No pictures."

I frowned, thrown off-track by her statement. "What?"

Kara pointed to the faded square patches on the walls, the cluster of bare hooks. "You don't have any pictures. No family photos?"

"I guess not."

She didn't press further, but she glanced behind us as I led her into the living room. There was a spare hoodie lying over the back of the couch, and I shrugged it on, pulling up the zipper.

"That's better," Kara mumbled, seemingly to herself.

"Sorry, I didn't catch that."

"Oh, nothing. Doesn't matter."

We wandered toward the staircase. As we reached the landing, I realized belatedly I was leading her in the direction of my bedroom.

She paused outside Kit's bedroom, poking her head in and smiling at the collection of colorful posters and the guitars arranged in the corner.

"Kit's, I take it?" At my nod, she said, "Your brother's really sweet." She leaned her head against the doorjamb as she spoke, and my heart ached. She looked so soft, so pretty. I wanted to reach out, but my hands remained firmly by my sides. "You guys seem close."

I nodded. "It's just the two of us, you know?"

"I do." She let out a soft sigh.

Before I could question the reason behind her sigh, she skirted around me and headed for the door at the end of the corridor. "What's through here?"

I came up behind her and leaned over the top of her head to nudge the door open so that she could peer inside. "My bedroom."

She blinked, looking apprehensive. "May I?"

"Go right ahead."

She slipped into the room. I glanced behind me at the empty hallway, to make sure that we were alone. After picking up the distant clatter of pots and pans, and the sound of Kit whistling to himself, I followed her.

KARA

My breath caught in my throat as I stepped over the threshold into Ronan's room. I could feel his presence at my back. He wasn't leaning into me or anything, but my body sensed him anyway. It was like my synapses had rewired themselves: I could feel him whenever he was standing nearby.

His scent was strongest in this part of the house. As I neared the rumpled bedspread, his distinctive smell grew even stronger.

It was delicious, and heady, and it made me want to rip off my clothes and turn to press my naked body against his.

Damn. I couldn't believe where my thoughts kept heading.

The curtains were partly closed. I reached out and pulled one of them open, letting a beam of light fall across the hardwood floor. Ronan watched me, his face shrouded in darkness.

"Not much to see, I'm afraid." His gaze flicked between the dresser to the bed and back again. "I left in kind of a hurry."

"I can see that." I swallowed. My eye was drawn to the walls—or rather, their emptiness. Just a vast expanse of bare white space...

"What are you thinking?" he murmured.

I fought not to react. He was right behind me. I could feel his hot breath against the side of my neck.

"I can see a question burning in your eyes," he said. "Tell me."

I reached out until my fingertips touched the nearest wall. "Don't you get tired of waking up to a load of empty space?"

He huffed a laugh, as if I'd surprised him with my query. "I guess I'm kind of used to it."

You don't have to be. I didn't say anything, just trailed my hand over the bare whiteness. "That's... sad."

"How so?"

I shrugged. I hadn't meant to say it out loud."First the pictures, now this..." Ronan curled his hand around mine. His fingers brushed over the space I'd just vacated, like we were doing a weird kind of dance. "Are you into art?"

"I guess." I allowed his hand to guide mine, higher and higher, until I was standing on tiptoe. "I make homewares for people in my pack. Cushions, rugs, pottery, that kind of thing. Sometimes I paint. It depends, really."

"On what?"

I giggled. With his longer arms, he could reach way higher than me. I teetered on the balls of my feet before giving up and slumping back against his chest. He slid his arm around my waist, catching me.

He didn't let go.

Suddenly, it became much harder to breathe normally. "Inspiration."

I felt him take a couple of breaths, processing what I'd just said. "Sounds like you're an artist to me."

"Oh yeah?" I turned in his grasp.

His other arm came up to join the first, holding me in place. His body language was loose, casual, but his eyes burned with a heat that made me shiver.

"Uh huh." His gaze tracked over my face.

I tilted up my head, hungry in a way I'd never been before today.

He touched the side of my face, cradling it loosely. I let my part, acting purely on instinct, and his eyes widened a fraction.

His index finger traced below my mouth and his thumb skimmed over my bottom lip, pressing down slightly. At the feel of his roughened skin against my flesh, I almost moaned out loud.

I wanted him to kiss me... I imagined how it would feel, when he did...

"Dinner!"

We sprang apart like we'd both received an electric shock. I was certain I was flushed all over. Ronan, for his part, just shook his head and a rumble filled his chest.

"My brother has great timing." He strode over to the door and held it open for me.

"I can hear that."

My body still felt like it was alive with electricity. How would I be able to concentrate on dinner now?

We made our way down to the kitchen without incident, although I felt Ronan's eyes on my face, particularly my mouth, the entire time we were getting settled at the table. Kit brought out a delicious-smelling stir-fry, and my mouth watered. I hadn't realized how hungry I was, until this moment.

"Thank you." I smiled up at him as he handed me a bowl. I didn't know whether it was the stress of the morning, or the close encounter in Ronan's bedroom, but I was ravenous.

"You're welcome." Kit's voice had a hint of smugness in it. When I looked up, he was eyeing Ronan with open amusement. "Did you get the full tour, Kara?"

"Kit." Ronan's sharp tone made his brother laugh out loud. "C'mon."

"It's okay." I winked at Ronan before turning my attention to Kit.

"Ronan showed me *everything,* including your secret stash hidden in your bedroom. So, who is she? One of the girls in your pack?"

Kit's mischievous expression switched to shock. "Wh-what?"

He hurried across the room, mumbling something about fetching the salt and pepper, before disappearing altogether. A few seconds later, we heard the tell-tale thud of footsteps rushing up the stairs.

Ronan raised an eyebrow at me. "What the hell was all that about? We didn't even go into his room."

"I know we didn't." I laughed. "But I know teenage boys, okay? If it's not a stash of love letters he's hiding up there, it's porn. Either way, I figure he'll leave us alone now."

Ronan's mouth fell open, and he spluttered with laughter. "Oh, *wow.* You're a genius."

"Nah." I ducked my head at the compliment, my face heating up all over again. "Just used to handling obnoxious younger brothers, is all."

Ronan said nothing, but his face was open and curious as he took another bite of food. The plates were stacked high. Like the men in my pack, Ronan and Kit could clearly put food away. I played with my fork before trying the food. It was as delicious as it smelled.

After several mouthfuls, I spoke. "I have a brother too." I picked up my glass and took a sip, keeping my eyes firmly fixed on Ronan. "His name's Jason."

"How much older are you?"

"Hmm... twelve minutes?" I laughed at the surprise in Ronan's face. "We're twins. I never let him forget that I'm the oldest, though."

Ronan shot me a grin, all sharp, white incisors. He must have been living in his shifter form for a long while, because I could see the wolf in him still. It had been hours since he'd shifted, but there it was, right near the surface.

Watching me.

I swallowed hard, and his eyes trailed down my throat, noting and tracking the motion.

Kit slid back into the room and took his seat at the table. At our questioning looks, he threw me a rueful smile. "Well played, new girl. Well played."

I inclined my head in a small bow.

"I like her." Kit sat back in his chair, folding his arms behind his head. He sat opposite Ronan, and I was struck by the family resemblance.

"Me too," Ronan murmured.

When I looked up at him, his pale amber eyes were fixed on me, with an expression so hungry that all coherent thoughts fled out of my head.

CHAPTER 6
KARA

By the time we finished dinner and returned to the town square, a huge bonfire was standing, half-built, in the middle of the clearing. A group of guys emerged, each carrying a vast log over his shoulders. They were all shouting with laughter and trying to shoulder-barge their friends so that they'd drop their cargo. At the site of the bonfire, they dumped the logs, with others bringing handfuls of kindling to add to the pyre.

Early evening had fallen. The sky above us was faded blue, and fireflies darted through the loose clusters of pack members who surrounded the pyre. The people's chatter and laughter filled the open air, growing louder as we approached.

A sharp pang pierced through me.

The atmosphere was familiar, and yet not. If I closed my eyes, I could imagine, just for a second, that I was back in my own pack, with the people I'd known my whole life, getting ready for an evening of celebration. I could almost reach out and touch them—the people who loved me just as fiercely as I loved them. My family.

Back where I belong.

And then the bubble of familiarity was gone and I was surrounded instead by strangers, on a rival pack's land, and the only people I knew here were Ronan, Kit and Elder Frey.

"Hey." Ronan moved his head closer to mine. Even over the noise of the gathering, his deep voice made my skin tingle. "We can head home if you want, get an early night. No-one would mind, I swear."

Home. He meant the Alpha's house. The place with the empty walls.

"I'm fine," I whispered. Then I said it again, a little louder, and found myself believing it.

I *would* be fine. I would make sure of it.

Ronan squeezed my fingers, so brief I barely had time to react. "Come on. I'll introduce you to some folks."

I let him lead me over to the log bearers, who all looked up as we approached. They were almost done with the bonfire. It was taller than I was by a good foot and a half. They were all panting with exertion, but they had bright smiles for both of us.

"What did you do to build this?" Ronan walked toward them, nodding at the structure. "Chop down half the forest?"

"I guess you'll never know, since you weren't here to help us," the nearest one shot back, before rushing over and pulling Ronan into a hug. "Where've you been, man?"

Ronan extracted himself and hooked his thumbs into his pockets, giving a loose shrug. The guy who had hugged Ronan didn't seem bothered by his lack of response. Instead, his gaze slid over and landed on me. Unlike Kit and Ronan, this guy's hair was sandy and short. A deep scar ran through his left brow.

"Aren't you gonna introduce us?" he said to Ronan, grinning at me.

Ronan sidled in close to me, as if he didn't like the other man's gaze on me. "Kara, this is Noah." He pointed to the shorter guy just behind. "That's Jake. And the guy with the burning torch is Zac."

Noah whirled around. "Zac!" He strode away from us with his hands flung wide. "C'mon, man, not cool! We were gonna light it up together, you know that!"

He and Zac started to bicker over the torch, which burnt out, unnoticed, between them. Ronan and I were breathless with laugher as we wandered away, weaving through the crowd.

"Are they always like that?"

"Pretty much, yeah." Ronan's eyes were soft, still glowing with amusement. "They're good guys. We grew up together. They never treated me any different for being the Alpha's son or anything, and I appreciate that. I know I can trust those three."

I thought of Allara. My best friend, the person who, aside from my brother, I knew the best out of anyone.

That was how I knew her—not as my Alpha, but first and foremost, as my friend. It was how I still thought of her. My *best* friend. Growing up, it had never occurred to me that she had a huge weight on her shoulders, an expectation that one day, she would follow in her father's footsteps.

When she ran off to the city, it had hurt. But I understood why she had done it. Now that she was back, it was as if she'd never left. I hoped that she felt about me as Ronan clearly did about his friends.

Trust in friendship was important, and rare, and when you found it, you had to hold onto it.

"Sure," I said eventually. I took Ronan's hand in mine like I'd done it a thousand times before. He looked down at our entwined fingers, surprise in his eyes, but he didn't let go.

Hand-in-hand, we made our way over to a long trestle table, where food and drinks were being laid out.

I became aware that we were being watched. A tall, willowy

woman stood nearby, leaning against a wall with her arms folded. Her eyes were fixed on us. When I glanced at her, she raised an eyebrow as if in challenge.

I froze. It couldn't be. But it was.

Naomi.

"Hey, what's wrong?" Ronan asked me.

I nodded over to where Naomi was standing. She hadn't taken her eyes off us. Her gaze remained challenging, like she was daring me to start something.

"What is *she* doing here?" I hissed.

Over the past few hours, I'd been growing more and more relaxed in this new environment. But one sight of Naomi was all it took to get my hackles back up.

"Wait, Naomi?" Ronan glanced in her direction, looking confused. "Do you know her?"

"Yes. We've met before."

Something in my tone must have registered my dislike, because his eyebrows crept toward his hairline. "Oh, this should be good."

"She used to visit our pack," I said. "She managed to get her claws into my brother Jason. He even considered making her his mate. When his *true* mate came along, she wasn't happy and she didn't care who knew it. I haven't seen her for months. It's just a shock, that's all."

Ronan let out a low whistle. "Damn. That sounds like Naomi all right."

I gave him a questioning look, and he shrugged.

"She's still a part of the Thornwood Clan, but only in name. She comes around here when she wants something. The rest of the time, she's out causing trouble somewhere else. Shifters, humans, who knows?" He shook his head. "Who cares? As long as she's not making trouble here..."

"I guess every pack has its own poison," I said, thinking of Jaime. "Though, if she's still considered Thornwood, then anything she does would reflect on your pack's reputation, wouldn't it?"

"Like Jaime and the Banes?"

Touché. Ronan was probably as responsible for Naomi's bad behavior, as Allara was for Jaime's. Which was to say, not at all. Naomi and Jaime, and others like them who behaved badly, were responsible for themselves. No one else could be blamed for any adult's poor life choices or decisions.

Naomi's lip curled in a sneer, as if she could hear the negative train of my thoughts. I turned away from her, determined to put the toxic woman out of my head.

Ronan and I lingered by the refreshment table. He poured me a drink of something sweet and fruity, and I sipped it as we turned back toward the center of the clearing. The bonfire was alight now, yellow tongues of flame creeping along the dry kindling, sending smoke into the sky.

We only look a couple of steps in the direction of the bonfire, before Naomi intercepted us.

"Kara." Her smooth voice set my teeth on edge. "Fancy running into you here. Long time no see."

I forced my features into a smile. "Indeed. Hello Naomi."

Without meaning to, I shrank into Ronan's side, as if my body already knew I would receive support from him, even if my head hadn't quite caught up. His hand tightened around mine.

Naomi's gaze flicked down to our joined hands, and her eyes widened slightly, as if she'd only just noticed.

Oh, come on. You clocked us from twenty feet away, bitch. Enough with the theatrics already.

"Oh, wow." Naomi let out a warm chuckle, but her eyes remained calculating. *Snake eyes.* "I see *you* didn't waste any time."

Don't rise to her bait. That's exactly what she wants.

"I'm here on business," I said, my voice tight. "Now, if you'll excuse us..."

"It sure doesn't look like it." Naomi folded her arms. The movement pushed her breasts forward, emphasizing her ample cleavage. She flicked a glance at Ronan as if checking to see if he'd noticed. My eyes narrowed. "How long has it been, a few hours? I have to say, Kara. I really didn't think you had it in you."

"Naomi." Ronan's voice was firm. An Alpha's command.

Naomi flinched a little, but then rallied. "I'm serious! You always seemed so... meek, so shy. Just like a sad little mouse, trailing around after me and your brother."

A deep rumble began in Ronan's chest, and I tugged quickly on his hand. *I've got this.* "Funny you should mention Jason." I tilted up my chin, meeting her narrowed gaze. "He and Tammy have a beautiful new baby. They're doing amazingly, all three of them. I've never seen my brother so happy. How are *you* doing, Naomi?"

Naomi opened her mouth, then closed it. Her face turned red and she swiveled and rushed away.

Good. She could choke on her own poisonous tongue for all I cared.

Ronan released a huff of laughter. "Remind me not to get on your bad side," he murmured, and I shrugged. All the grief that woman had given Jason, and the empty promises she'd made, was all in the past. She would never be able to hurt him again.

Together, Ronan and I made our way toward the bonfire.

"You okay?" Ronan bent his head close to mine. His eyes were full of concern.

I nodded. "I'm fine. I can handle her."

He glanced behind us with a furrowed brow. "I'm sure you can. You just proved that. Only, be careful with her, okay? She doesn't take kindly to insults. I've seen her strike back, and strike hard. I don't want that to happen to you."

I looked up at him, warmed all the way through by his concern. "I will be careful. I promise."

I have no intention of going anywhere near that bitch.

His face smoothed out at my expression, and he softened, putting an arm around me. His arm felt good over my shoulders, warm and protective.

"I guess we should make the rounds," he said. "That's the sort of thing one does at a party, right?"

"You don't sound stoked at the prospect. Aren't Alpha's supposed to be extroverted and genial?"

His answering glower made me laugh; I leaned into his body and slid an arm around his waist.

"I'm just teasing," I whispered. "You'll be a great Alpha; you've got the command needed for the job. You got this."

CHAPTER 7
RONAN

Attending a party thrown in honor of my return and ascendancy to Alpha wasn't high up on the list of ways I wanted to spend my time.

Having Kara by my side made things even harder. Everywhere I turned, I caught curious glances. I could see people's minds turning over, wondering what could possibly have happened at the meeting house, and why she was now pressed into my side as if we were joined at the hip.

As if we were mates.

Kara seemed to shy away from the attention almost as much as I did.

To my relief, however, people mostly left us alone. The other members of the pack had been told by Kit that I wouldn't be answering any questions tonight about where I'd been. I felt Naomi's eyes burning into my back more than a couple of times, but I was careful to evade her.

I did not want my first job as Alpha to be stopping a fight between that annoying woman, and Kara.

I was given the prime spot in front of the bonfire, with Kara beside me, on the low wooden bench that my mother and father used to sit at, watching over the rest of the clan. For once, I didn't refuse the honor. I could see that Kara was more rattled by Naomi's sudden appearance than she was letting on, so we sat on the prime bench and people-watched for a while.

My thigh felt warm where it pressed against hers.

"That's my Aunt Clarissa, and my young cousin Molly." I pointed out the two redheads as they passed, giving little Molly a wave. She giggled and ducked behind her mom, but her tiny hand stuck out from behind Clarissa's legs, waving back.

I talked Kara through the dynamics of our clan: who was considering who for a potential mate, which ones were competing, who had broken up, and the couples who were fated for each other. As I discovered, it was a perfect mirror of her own clan. All the rivalries and friendships that made up the rich tapestry of a shifter pack, were laid out for all to see, and though the people may have been different, the dynamics within my pack, and hers, were pretty much the same.

"Let me get this straight." Kara laughed. "Noah was with Lacey, but then he broke up with her for Ruby, but when Lacey started dating Jake, Noah wanted *Lacey* again? How does that work? So, who does Lacey want?"

I groaned and dropped my head into my hands. "Ugh. When you put it like that, it sounds even crazier."

"And I thought our pack was dramatic." Kara smiled, her gaze drifting toward the glow of the bonfire. "This is lovely," she said, and a warm feeling grew in my chest.

There were so many stories, so much I didn't yet know about her. I wanted to know everything.

We have time.

Kara wasn't going anywhere, after all. As I remembered the deal we'd struck, the warmth inside me mingled with a twinge of uncertainty.

She's only here because she has to be, remember? The moment you allow her to leave, she'll be home to the Bane clan in a shot.

"So, what about you?" Kara's hand on my arm jolted me back to the present. "Where are you in all this drama?"

"Nowhere," I answered truthfully. "I steered clear of all that. I had the occasional fling with human women, but nothing serious."

"Human." She looked surprised. "Why specifically human and not another shifter?"

I chuckled. "Yeah, I guess it sounds a bit strange. But with shifters, everything gets so... messy. All the pheromones and hormones flying everywhere. I've seen first-hand what kind of chaos it can create. I didn't want to risk my position like that, not over some casual hook-up."

Kara was silent, staring into the flames. From the moment I saw her, I thought she was beautiful, but in the dusk and the firelight, she looked extra stunning. Her dark hair pooled around her shoulders, and her eyes glimmered. I resisted the urge to reach out and tuck a soft strand behind her ear, to stroke a finger over the delicate blush on her cheeks.

"What about you?" I said instead, scrambling for a distraction. "You must have had offers from many of the men in your pack. Or other shifters passing through the area, perhaps?"

I struggled to keep the jealousy out of my voice at the thought of other shifters around her, competing for her attention, for the chance to mate.

"Yes, there were a couple, I guess." Kara bit her lip, sounding evasive. She shrugged. "Your parents must have wanted you to find a match. You were the future Alpha, after all."

Now it was my turn to dodge the question.

"They did," I said shortly. "But, like I said, it never interested me."

But that was before.

Now Kara was here, and I couldn't deny that her presence had changed everything.

"Kit was always the extrovert," I said. "Even with the age gap, he was always the one following in Dad's footsteps. He's more cut out for the Alpha role, than I'll ever be."

I'd always preferred to be off exploring the forest with my friends than learning about pack politics. Now that I was older, I'd learned to mask how uncomfortable I felt when people looked to me as their leader, but that was all it was—a mask.

Deep down, underneath the mask, I knew it should have been Kit who was the first born. The Alpha.

"He just needed a few more years to mature, and he'd have been a perfect leader for the pack, but unfortunately we weren't given that opportunity with the passing of our father."

Kara seemed to read my thoughts exactly. The firelight flickered in her gorgeous eyes, and I drew a sharp breath when she took my hand and our fingers tangled together.

"Look, I know my opinion doesn't mean much to you." She drew a shaky breath, continuing before I could argue. "We don't really know each other that well—hell, I'm not even supposed to be here at all—but from where I'm standing, I think what you just said is a load of crap."

My mouth dropped open. Whatever I'd been expecting, it wasn't *that.*

"What?"

She tilted up her chin, her expression full of defiance. In this light, she was a far cry from the quiet, withdrawn girl I'd met that morning. "I've seen how people look at you around here. They respect you; look up to you. They listen when you talk. And the way you talk about them! You care about them, Ronan. Their wellbeing, their wants, their fears. That's what's important. Being an Alpha is about so much more than being the life and soul of the party. I was joking before, when I said an Alpha is usually extroverted. That's a plus, but its not a requirement for the job. Commanding respect, and having the ability to lead in a clear and rational manner, is what people need, in their leader."

She let out a huff, and her shoulders slumped. Her bottom lip trembled, like she was on the verge of pouting at me.

She was adorable.

I couldn't resist any longer. I reached out and tucked that loose piece of hair behind her ear. She turned her face toward my palm, closing her eyes as if in bliss at my touch, before flushing deep red and jerking away.

"I'm so sorry," she mumbled, covering her face with her hands. "I don't know what that was."

"Hey." I tried unsuccessfully to pry her hands away from her face. "C'mon, it's okay!"

She lowered her hands to her lap. Her gaze darted down to the cup of punch I'd poured for her earlier, resting on the bench beside her.

"Did you spike my drink?" Her mouth curled up at one side to let me know she was joking.

"I can assure you, I didn't." I spread my hands wide. "That was all you."

"Uh huh." She tilted her head to one side. "I'm onto you, Thornwood."

"Is that right?" I leaned closer. From this distance, I could smell her intoxicating scent underneath the smoke from the fire.

I tilted my head to mirror hers. We were inches away from each other. I couldn't tell if the rapid drumbeat I heard was my heart or hers.

A loud *whoop* sounded from nearby, and a light rain of punch fell all around us. Some of it got on Kara, but most of it fell on me. We jolted apart, and I stood up, enraged.

"Oops," Noah called from nearby. "Sorry, Ronan! My bad."

Kara stood up too, her hand falling onto my arm. She must have seen my expression, because she laughed. "It's no big deal."

She stood up on her tiptoes and whispered, "It was getting just a tad hot there, for a bit."

I looked down at her. She had a small, secretive smile on her face, and her thumb rubbed back and forth over my arm, light and teasing.

"We could just head back to your place." She raised her eyebrows. "And get a change of clothes."

Oh.

"Good idea." I returned her smile.

The walk back to the house was thick with a different sort of tension than earlier. Every time her hand brushed against mine, I wanted to grab her right then and there, pin her up against the side of the nearest building, and claim her as mine.

I clenched my hands into fists and forced myself to keep moving. We sped up our pace as the house came into view around the next corner. The street was dark and deserted; it appeared that everyone was still at the bonfire.

By the time we reached the stairs of the porch, I couldn't handle the need anymore. I *needed* to kiss her, to hold her, to drown in her essence. Kara had one foot on the top step when I grabbed her and spun her round so fast that she gasped.

We stood there, drunk on each other. I could tell from her somnolent features that she felt the same way as me. The full moon above us lit her face perfectly. I drank in every detail: her wide eyes, her parted, full mouth. Her lips, crying out for mine.

She surged up and dragged my mouth to hers.

I groaned and hitched her up. We stumbled across the porch, and I pressed her back against the front door.

The kiss grew in urgency, deeper and hotter than before. I

groaned as our tongues slid against each other, my hands on either side of her head. She submitted eagerly, tilting her head up and arching her body against mine.

Why had I ever thought she would be too timid? Afraid of my passion?

She was ready and willing, and I couldn't wait to explore more of her body.

The wolf in me wanted to take her, right here, right now, under the night sky and the stars sparkling above us.

The man knew better. She deserved more than a quick fuck. Kara deserved everything I had to give, and more.

I reached around her and pushed open the door, guiding her over the threshold and into the darkened house.

KARA

We stumbled through the door and somehow made it into the lounge, pressing kisses onto every inch of skin we could reach.

It was dark, but we managed to reach the dark shape of the sofa, more by instinct than anything else. I collapsed back onto the cushions and Ronan fell on me like a starving man. He suckled on my lower lip, taking it between his teeth, and I gasped.

The gasp turned to a whimper as his hands slid up over my shirt, skating over my ribs, cupping my breasts. His touch felt so good. I needed to get closer.

Ronan moved back and grabbed my jeans, tugging them down my legs so there was nothing between us but my damp panties and his jeans that barely held in his erection.

Then he was back, kissing me, stealing my reason. But I had to tell him the truth...

"I lied," I gasped. "There's never—I've never—"

"What are you trying to say?"

I shuddered at the sound of his voice—half wolf, half man. The shifter was there, right at the surface, and it wanted to claim its mate.

I knew, because mine was right there, ready to leap out and claim my mate, too.

I shook my head, moaning, overwhelmed by his touch, and most of all by the sensation of his tongue dragging over my skin.

It was almost impossible to concentrate. His tongue trailed over my bare stomach, lighting up my nerve endings like a switchboard. Still, I had to get this out. I persisted, somehow, between gasps and moans. "I've never—never done this before."

Ronan went still.

He looked up. His face was unreadable in the dark, but his eyes glinted with arousal. I shivered, wanting his body on mine but not knowing how to ask for it. I settled for squirming and arching my back, trying to encourage his mouth to return to feasting on me, but he shifted away so that we were no longer touching.

I bit back a whine at the loss.

"What do you mean?" He was breathing heavily, short, punched-out breaths. Or was that me? I couldn't tell any more. We were both breathing so hard I could barely hear anything else.

"I've just... I've never." I turned my face into the couch cushion to avoid his piercing gaze. "*You* know."

He sat back completely, slumping down against the back of the sofa. "You've never been with a man before."

I squeezed my eyes shut, nodding.

He was silent. I lay there in the dark, breathing in and out and trying not to panic. Why was he suddenly so quiet?

"Time for bed." The softness of Ronan's voice startled me into awareness once more.

I jerked my head up. My hair, I could feel, was all over the place, but I couldn't bring myself to care. I was too shocked. "What?"

"It's time for bed," Ronan said slowly, like I hadn't heard him the first time.

"With... you?"

"No."

But... I'm not tired." I sat up and slid across the couch until I was pressed up against his side. He didn't reach for me, but he didn't shift away, either. I dropped my head and kissed his shoulder, the side of his neck, sliding my thighs until I was straddling one of his knees. I kissed the side of his neck again, groaning and clenching my thighs around his leg.

A tiny groan slipped past his lips, but that was the only sign he was as affected by our closeness as me.

Gently but firmly, he took my shoulders in his hands and pushed me back.

"*I* am."

From the sound of his voice, he was anything but tired, but his jaw was set and firm. I tried to rock forward into his lap again. His arms tensed around me, and all of a sudden, I was up off the couch, cradled in his thick arms.

"Ronan!" My feet flailed in the air, but it was no use. He carried me across the room, heading toward the stairs. "Ronan, put me *down*."

He ignored me, climbing the stairs and heading in the direction of his bedroom. *Maybe he'd changed his mind?*

My heart started hammering, jackrabbit fast, when we reached the threshold, but when he deposited me on his bed he didn't climb in after me. He just stood there, one hand rubbing at the back of his neck as he stared down at me.

"You can sleep here tonight." His gruff voice, such a stark contrast from his warm, easy tones earlier, shocked me. "I'll take the spare room down the hall."

He crossed over to the door.

"Ronan!"

At the sound of my high-pitched, desperate cry, he turned his head. I sat up in the middle of the bed, panting.

I felt shameless, but it was no use. My breath hitched as something like a sob escaped me.

"Please…"

Holding his gaze, I let my legs fall open. I stared at him imploringly.

Don't leave me here like this.

In a flash, he was at the foot of the bed. His hands circled my ankles and dragged me to the edge of the mattress. I moaned at the sight of his mussed hair between my thighs. My jeans were long gone, abandoned somewhere. His hands climbed up my shins, over my knees, my thighs, mapping every inch of skin. His hot, panting breath huffed against my bare skin, and my core throbbed with need.

"You want this?" he rumbled, and I whined out loud, feeling the vibration of his voice more than I heard his words.

"Yes," I moaned. "I can't—"

"Shh." Ronan buried his face in the soft part of my thigh, teeth scraping the sensitive, overheated flesh. "I've got you."

He slid his mouth up higher, over my panties, and I almost screamed out loud when I felt the first sweep of his tongue over the center of my pussy. Even through the sheer fabric barrier between his mouth and my skin, it was almost too much.

My hips tried to ride forward but he pinned me in place, his broad hands firm on either side of my hips holding me spread-eagled. I sobbed and squirmed, but he was relentless in his teasing, circling my clit with his tongue until I bucked and thrashed.

He pulled away for a brief moment, giving me just enough time to catch my breath, before he dove forward once more and took me in his mouth.

By the time he pulled back yet again, my face was on fire and I was on the verge of tears. I took one heaving breath after another, trying to gather myself.

I knew that, with one word from me, it would all be over.

But I didn't want that. I wanted this agony to go on forever, if it meant that Ronan kept his hands on me.

He slid my panties aside and spread me apart with his fingers. My hands clenched and unclenched in the bedsheets. Now that he'd relinquished his hold on me, I was free to move, to push my hips forward to where they wanted to be.

I did just that, back and forth over his tongue. After all the teasing, it was heaven, pleasure like I'd never known, and nothing stopped me from taking all of it for myself.

When my climax finally hit, it was almost a shock; I'd been on the precipice for so long that when I finally tumbled over the edge I could do nothing but hang on for the ride as Ronan wrung wave after wave of ecstasy out of me.

At last I collapsed back onto the bedsheets, utterly exhausted.

In a weakened daze, I reached out for the fuzzy shape that was Ronan. He pulled away from me; this time, it was gentle, almost reluctant.

I was just present enough to see him leave the room, softly closing the door behind him, before my exhaustion took over and I slipped into unconsciousness.

CHAPTER 8

RONAN

I woke with a sore neck, a sore and aching groin, and a whole heap of guilt.

Groaning, I shuffled around on my bed, trying to find a less lumpy part of the old mattress. Eventually I gave up and sat upright, shaking my hair out of my eyes.

My head gave a throb, and I winced, pressing a hand against my temple.

Damn. I didn't even drink that much last night.

I chalked it up to the stress of being in human form, after spending so long as a wolf. My body was still calibrating itself, reorienting to the environment.

And, of course, to the base need that had roared through my system half the night, every time I relived Kara's gasping cries as she climaxed beneath my mouth. Those remembered cries prevented me from getting to sleep until the early hours of the morning.

I rolled up and out of bed, pulled on a pair of old jeans and a t-shirt, and stumbled my way toward the kitchen. When I passed something on the floor in the lounge, I scooped it up and my fingers closed around the crumpled pile of fabric. I lifted it, holding it up to the light.

Kara's sweater. She must have dropped it last night, while we were...

I closed my eyes, letting the sweater fall back to the floor. Her scent clung in the air around me; my cock stirred yet again at the memory of her in this exact spot the night before, and then after that, in my bedroom...

Now I knew exactly what she looked like when she came. I glanced up at the ceiling. My room lay directly above the lounge, and I listened carefully for any signs of life.

The house was totally silent. It looked like I was the first one up.

In more ways than one.

I groaned out loud before clambering to my feet and slinking off in the direction of a cold shower.

I took advantage of the early start, busying myself with preparing breakfast. By the time I heard signs of life coming from upstairs, I had a stack of pancakes ready on the table, and I was slicing up strawberries while I waited for the last pancake to be done.

Kit wandered in first, yawning widely. The sight of him was a shock. I'd almost forgotten he lived here. I'd been so focused on Kara and what we had almost done last night.

"Hey man."

"Hey." I jabbed the spatula toward him in warning as he reached for a pancake. "Use a plate. And leave some for our guest."

Left to his own devices, Kit would just shove the whole thing into his mouth and then dive in for more. But we had company this morning, and I wanted to make a good impression.

That is, if I haven't squandered the opportunity already.

As if she'd heard my thoughts, Kara appeared in the doorway. She looked between us shyly, and I gave her an encouraging smile.

"You hungry?"

She nodded, sitting down opposite Kit and helping herself to a pancake. I nodded to Kit as we watched her fill the pancake with strawberries and roll it up neatly.

"See?" I turned back to the stove and slid the final pancake onto an empty plate, then wandered over to the table and sat beside her. "Manners."

"Whatever." Kit stuck his tongue out at me. "What did you guys get up to last night, anyway? I totally lost track of you, and by the time I got back here, it was dead quiet."

I looked at Kara, and she looked at me. We both started to speak at the same time.

"We were just—"

"We decided to take a walk and—"

"Stargazing." Kara's voice was firm and steady. "We were stargazing."

"Oh." Kit grabbed another pancake and slathered it with an unholy amount of maple syrup. "Cool."

"Cool," I echoed, meeting Kara's eyes and giving her a soft, secretive smile.

~

Just as we were wrapping up breakfast, we were interrupted by a volley of knocks on the front door. I excused myself from the table and went to answer it, only to find Noah, Jake, and Zac waiting for me with identical expressions of excitement.

I looked between the three of them. "What's up, guys?"

"Hunting season is what's up, man!" Noah reached out and cuffed me on the shoulder. "C'mon, we're heading into the forest on guard duty. We were gonna grab something to eat on the way back. You coming, or what? Been a while since you joined us."

I glanced behind me toward the kitchen, where Kit and Kara were still sitting, finishing up.

Patrolling, followed by a hunt? How long will that take?

It stood to reason that my friends—brothers in spirit, if not in blood—would expect me to keep to my regular duties like nothing had changed. But the truth was, everything had changed. Like Noah said, I'd been gone for some time, and...

The memory of Kara's sweet face, the way she'd gazed up at me last night, was enough to harden my resolve.

"I'm kind of in the middle of something right now." I started to draw the door closed, shaking my head. "Sorry. I'll take the flack from the Elders, okay? Don't worry about it. I'll join you next time."

Jake nudged his foot into the gap before I could shut the door completely. "Ronan, c'mon. You've been AWOL for weeks, and now you don't even wanna *hunt*? What's wrong with you, man?"

In unison, I was met with three pairs of wide, dejected eyes. Guilt prickled inside me. Here I was, abandoning guard duty with my pack mates, after everything I'd put them through...

A voice sounded in the back of my head. The last voice I wanted to think of right now: my father.

Remember your duty, Ronan.

What the hell *was* my duty? Things had gotten so muddled... I pressed my fist against the side of the door, one foot on the threshold, torn.

Soft footsteps sounded behind me, and Kara appeared at my elbow.

She smiled at the three visitors, then directed her gaze at me. "Can I talk to you for a sec, Ronan?"

"Sure." I moved away from the door, leaving it open. Out of the corner of my eye, I watched Zac slump down onto the decking. The other two leaned against the doorframe, their downcast mood obvious.

"I think you should go with them," Kara whispered, once we were in the other room.

My mouth fell open. "What? You heard all that?"

Kara's mouth tilted up at the corner. "Your friends weren't exactly whispering. Also…"

She raised an eyebrow.

Right. Shifter hearing.

I was so used to dating only human women. I kept forgetting that Kara had the wolf in her. Gentle and breakable as she seemed, I knew there was a tough core underneath the soft, sweet exterior. Every so often she let it show. Perhaps that seeming gentleness made her stronger than many others, rather than weak. She clearly had control of her shifter side.

"Are you sure?" Something twanged in my chest at the thought of leaving her here without me. What if something happened to her? "I can send them away."

"You have your duty," Kara said, like it was as simple as that. "And I have mine. Go. I'll still be here when you get back."

"You better," I grumbled.

"Absence makes the heart grow fonder, you know."

"Hmm. So they say."

She huffed a laugh and reached up to drag my head down toward hers.

The kiss was short and chaste, nothing like the fiery passion from last night. Nevertheless, pure need pulsed through me, hot and greedy, just from the brief contact.

When we pulled apart, her eyes were full of challenge.

"I'll see you later." Her words dripped with intent.

I wanted to devour her. Again.

With a deep sigh, I stepped back from her and headed for the door.

~

Kara

Once Ronan was gone, I found myself at a loose end.

Kit disappeared shortly afterwards. It was a weekday, and he said he had a study group with some of the other teenagers in the pack. After a brief internal debate, I decided to slip outside and head out to the town square once again.

After all, I had a job to do. A purpose, a reason I was here.

I tucked away the memory of Ronan's intense, hungry gaze. For now, at least, I had to be vigilant. I was here as an ambassador, after all. It made sense to get to know as many people as I could, and try and establish some rapport within the pack.

The thought made my heart sink. I was a loner by nature, far more comfortable with my paintbrushes than with making small talk.

Luckily for me, I ran into a familiar face almost immediately. And it wasn't Naomi, thank goodness.

Halfway down the road that led to the meeting house, a small vegetable patch lay between two cottages. Elder Frey waved me over, one hand resting on his spade and the other wiping his brow.

"Good morning, Kara!" His face broadened into a smile as I grew closer, and he beckoned me forward. "Come in, come in, don't be shy."

Hesitantly, I slipped open the wooden gate and picked my way over the narrow gravel path that ran between the raised beds. Broad beans trailed off on pitched wooden frames, and a grapevine crept on a trellis over the back wall. Elder Frey was in the middle of the patch, pulling out weeds from a bed of frothy green stems. Once I got close enough, he tossed me a pair of spare gloves.

"Anything that looks like it doesn't belong," he said, pulling up a dandelion and holding it up to demonstrate, before tossing it into a nearby wheelbarrow, "just root it out."

I pulled on the gloves and got to work beside him. We worked in companionable silence for a few minutes until he sat back on his heels, turning to face me.

"So, are you settling in around here? I know it's only been a short time, but are you comfortable?"

I nodded. "I am, actually. Surprisingly." I glanced around at the peaceful garden. Somewhere in the distance, I could hear faint laughter, and a gentle breeze rustled through the plants around us. There were many things that reminded me of my own pack village— enough that I didn't feel completely out of place. "When I first arrived, everything seemed so...different. But I think I might have been letting my nerves rule, at that point."

"The Bane Clan certainly have their way of doing things, and we have ours." Elder Frey nodded. "There are differences, of course, which is natural, but there are also many things that remain similar in most shifter communities. I hope that the Thornwood brothers are making you feel welcome in the Alpha's house."

"Yeah, they're great." I couldn't help but smile as I thought back to the morning. "Kit and Ronan... they remind me of my brother and I. The gentle ribbing, but underneath, they really care for each other."

"And you have everything you need?"

You could say that. I didn't answer, but the flush that I could feel cresting my cheeks told the story without me wanting to share it.

"Kara..." The Elder's face furrowed as his expression turned pensive; solemn. "I consider it my duty to tell you this, and I hope you will accept my advice. I assure you I speak only as a friend. I knew your Alpha's father very well, and I know he would want me to look out for one of his own."

I pulled my hands back from the vegetable patch and frowned, confused. "Tell me what?"

"What happened yesterday, between you and Ronan."

For a wild second, I thought he was referring to the night I'd spent in Ronan's bed. Then I realized he meant before, in the meeting house. *Oh.*

"I didn't want to say anything then. I didn't think it was my place."

"You mean... the fact that we seem to be fated?" I was totally puzzled as to what the Elder might be about to say.

Is being fated to a mate a bad thing? Where's he going with this?

Elder Frey looked regretful. He heaved a deep sigh, and for some reason the sound sent a chill creeping down my spine. Whatever he was about to say next, I wasn't sure I wanted to hear it.

"How many men have you known, Kara?" He spoke kindly, but his words didn't reassure me. "Not many, I'm willing to bet. A handful in your own pack, perhaps. And Ronan is the only one who has ever elicited these... feelings?"

"Nobody has even come *close*." I felt like it wasn't his business, but equally, I felt the need to be honest.

Whatever brief, passing interest I'd had for anyone else, none of them could hold a candle to the way I felt around Ronan.

"But," the Elder pressed, "given your—forgive me—lack of experience, who's to say that there isn't someone else out there? After all, how are you to know? Perhaps these feelings are an infatuation. One that, over time, will fade."

"Why are you saying this?" I bit out. I didn't understand his motive. My hands trembled, and anxiety sent my senses reeling. "I don't want anyone else. I don't—"

"Kara." Elder Frey's hand on my shoulder steadied me enough to take several deep breaths, and I felt my heart settle inside my chest. "I'm so sorry, my dear. I didn't mean to upset you."

"Well," I snapped, "you did."

"I can see that." There was a note of genuine regret in his voice. "Look, the bond between fated mates is a mysterious phenomenon. Nobody truly understands how it works. We only have the word of the individuals who experience it. All that those on the outside see more often than not, are two people who rush into a lifelong commitment without thinking through the long-term consequences."

"He hasn't promised me anything." I sniffed. "If that's what you're worried about."

"All I'm worried about is *you*."

Why is he only worried about me? What about his Alpha? Shouldn't he be worried about Ronan? Is there something about Ronan that he's not telling me? Something that might change my opinion about this whole situation, if I found out?

"I've told you, I'm fine." My voice wobbled. *Don't cry, dammit. Don't you dare cry.* "Look. I know that this is a curveball. I get it. This is your future Alpha, and I'm some stranger who showed up out of nowhere. But I promise you, the last thing I want to do is stand between him and his destiny."

I stood up shakily and brushed the soil off my jeans. Elder Frey looked up at me. In the glare of the midday sun, I couldn't read his expression.

"Just think about what I said, Kara." His soft voice wasn't soothing any more. I didn't want to listen or think. I just wanted to get away as fast as possible. "There are things you don't know. Some shifters... they just aren't meant to have a mate."

I'd heard enough. I mumbled something unintelligible in response and ran back through the garden, letting the gate clang shut behind me.

He didn't try to stop me.

I ran all the way back to the Thornwood house, tears blurring my eyes the whole way.

I waited until I was inside, safe and secure with the door locked behind me, before I finally let my tears fall.

CHAPTER 9

RONAN

Despite my initial reluctance to join my friends, we ended up staying out in the forest for most of the day.

It felt good to be back in shifter form, but not to be alone this time. To feel the wind through my fur, the dirt under my paws. After so long spent as an outcast—albeit self-imposed—having my packmates surrounding me again was nothing short of exhilarating. The joy of running with friends sang through my bone marrow, and when I put my head up and howled, snatches of their own song echoed back to me through the trees.

By the time I arrived back in town, I was spent. I shoved on the spare clothes we'd stashed in the gatehouse earlier, dressing in a daze. Noah nudged my shoulder as he wandered past.

He grabbed a bottle of water off the side of the gatehouse, chugging half of it in one go and wiping his mouth. "Tell us about the chick."

Jake bobbed up beside him and snagged the bottle for himself, ignoring Noah's protests. "Yeah, man! She's *hot.*"

My eyes narrowed and my teeth bared, lips peeled back to reveal my sharp incisors. My shifter growled; it was a struggle to wrestle it back down beneath the surface.

"Whoa." Zac appeared with spiky hair and a towel draped around his neck. He'd fallen into the creek as we were heading back and was none too pleased about it. "Dude, relax."

I shrugged off the guys as they attempted to calm me. "She's not just a *chick.* She's..." I hesitated, not sure how to explain Kara, and they seemed to get the message. Crowding me only made it harder to control the wolf within. It was easier when all of them backed off a touch.

"Wow," Noah whispered. He looked awed. "You're *actually* fated mates. Everyone was gossiping about it last night, but I didn't think it was true."

I didn't reply. The look on my face must have said enough, because the other two dropped down to a nearby bench, dumbfounded.

"We thought it was just a crush or something," Noah said. I stared at him with a raised brow, and he shrugged. "What? It seemed kinda far-fetched, is all."

"Is that why you're all tensed up?" Jake asked. "Man, you need to get it out of your system. All the crazy shifter stuff—it won't go away until you... you know."

"No," I rumbled. "I *don't* know."

Jake and Zac looked a little nervous. Noah came over and laid a hand on my arm. I didn't try to throw him off, but I did glare, hoping that the sheer force of my rage would get him to back off.

Ha. As if I'm ever that lucky. Noah has a set of balls the size of coconuts.

"What we're trying to say is..." Noah quirked an eyebrow, fixing me with his serious, steady gaze. "Don't try to fight this one, Ronan. I know how stubborn you get, but you just gotta let fate do its thing. The rest will fall into place. You'll see."

I grit my teeth, but managed to nod.

I want to see her. Right now.

It was the oddest thing, like a magnet dragging a compass needle due north—the urge to get back to her, now that I was close by, was almost overwhelming.

I left them soon afterwards, but only after I'd endured as many encouraging backslaps as I could handle.

I approached my house in good spirits.

The day had been more fun than I expected, but the conversation after had set my mind on one thing.

Kara.

From the look in her eyes as I left that morning, I was certain that she wanted to take things to the next level.

I wanted to go slow, to take my time with her. She was a virgin, and that state needed to be protected. Valued. Enjoyed. My shifter wanted to rush in, to claim, to devour.

Time would tell which instinct would win out.

I unlocked the door of the house and slipped inside, heading for the living room. At the sight of Kara's dark head resting at the edge of the sofa, my heart leapt.

She looked up as I moved closer, and I almost froze in place. Her eyes were red-rimmed, and she was pale. She sat up and curled her hands over her knees as I sat down beside her. Instead of meeting my gaze, she hung her head.

"What's wrong?"

My mind flashed through a thousand possibilities. I wanted to demand answers, to ask who did this. Who made her miserable?

"Hey." I reached over, putting my hand on her cheek. She let me tilt her face upwards readily enough, but her gaze skittered away from mine. "Talk to me. Did someone do something to upset you? Hurt you?"

She shook her head and wiped a hand over her face. "No, I'm fine. It's nothing like that."

"Doesn't look like it." I took her hand between mine, turning her palm over and pressing a kiss against it. She let out a soft sigh, so I did it again. "C'mon. Tell me."

"I'm just..." Her voice trembled. I thought she was about to burst into tears, but she didn't. She steeled herself before continuing. "I'm scared of this. Of *us*. What if it's not... right?"

Not right? My heart beat in alarm. "What do you mean?"

"I mean..." Kara shook her head. Her dark hair fell in a curtain of loose waves, hiding her face. "We barely know each other. I don't want to... pressure you, or..."

I sat back. Realization was dawning on me, slow and sure. She didn't understand if this really was a fated mates situation. I wracked my brain for something to say. Some way to make her see how certain I was about this. About her.

Even at the best of times, words were never my strong suit.

I stood up from the sofa, and she looked up sharply.

"Wait here," I said. "I want to show you something."

KARA

I curled my feet into the sofa cushions and pressed my head back against the couch, closing my eyes.

I thought of the soft, thick, woven blanket that I had at home. I'd made it with wool I'd dyed myself, in bright orange, red and purple. My favorites. The colors of a sunset.

A tear slid down my cheek.

I wiped it away impatiently. There was no sense being homesick. I was fine.

The things that Elder Frey had said haunted me. His words had been going round and round in my mind since this morning; by the time Ronan had come home, I'd been half-convinced I'd be sent packing immediately.

But Ronan hadn't done that. He'd kissed me, and spoken in a soft, soothing voice.

Then he'd disappeared again. The minute I thought I'd gotten a handle on him, he did something like that; just took off without a word.

I wonder if I'll ever work him out.

I wonder if he'll ever give me the chance.

I squeezed my eyes shut and focused on breathing. Several thuds came from upstairs, like he was rummaging around for something.

A few minutes later, I heard him back in the doorway. I opened my eyes and saw him standing there, with a slender black file tucked under his arm. In spite of my low mood, my curiosity was piqued. I sat up straighter as he dropped down beside me.

His face was unreadable as he pulled out the file and held it to me. At first I just blinked at it, uncertain.

"Here." He brandished the file until I eventually took it. He tapped the cover, eyes flicking between me and it. "Open it."

"What's this?"

"Just open it. Please."

I opened the folder. As soon as I laid eyes on its contents, I let out a small, involuntary breath.

A loose pile of photographs was tucked inside. I picked up the top one and held it to the light, my pulse racing.

"Is that..." I trailed off, looking at him questioningly. "You?"

He nodded.

I stared at the tiny child in the photograph. His head was thrown back in uproarious laughter. The woman carrying him was smiling too, a broad, wide smile that crinkled the corners of her eyes.

I pointed at her. "This is your mom?"

"Yes."

I looked down at the photo, then up at Ronan. "You have the same eyes."

Ronan smiled sadly. He took the photo from me and tucked it into the back of the pile.

We shuffled through the rest of the photos together. There were more shots of him, a little older, barefoot and wild, holding baby Kit's chubby hand in the forest. On the shoulders of a tall, bearded man; cuddled up on the sofa with his brother; running with his pack-mates in the woods. And laughing—always laughing.

Ronan held up another picture. "Here. This was the one I wanted to show you."

Ronan's mom and dad stared up at us from the photograph. They were seated on the front porch of a house. I recognized it as the one we were in. The wooden beams were neatly painted, and their smiles were shy, but their eyes were bright and glowing with happiness. His mom wore a lace veil and had a bouquet of wildflowers in her hands. His dad's hair was smoothed down, and aside from the beard, he looked very much like Ronan.

"This was taken after their bonding ceremony." Ronan's voice was low and hushed. I leaned in closer. "My grandma took it. Mom and her were just visiting the pack. They lived a couple of states over, in another pack at the edge of the city. But Dad took one look at my mom and she looked at him, and that was it. She was the one for him. His one true mate."

My eyes met his. Even in the low light, they were such a piercing shade of amber. For a split second, I lost my breath.

"Were they happy?" I asked, mostly to distract myself from the beauty of his eyes.

"Yeah." Ronan took the photo back and closed the file, setting it down on the coffee table. "Very happy. Everyone thought they were crazy, bonding with each other so soon after they met. But they didn't care what anyone else thought. They knew it was right."

I didn't know what to say. For some reason, I found that I was on the verge of tears. Without looking up, I reached out blindly and took his hand, tangling our fingers together.

"Thank you for sharing that with me." I finally got the courage to look at him, blinking away my blurred vision. "I would've liked to meet them."

"No problem." Ronan squeezed my hand. "I just wanted to show you... my parents couldn't help the way they felt. And neither can I, Kara. I know that what we have is real. No-one else can weigh in on that. I don't know if someone said something, or if the doubts you were having stem from you and no one else. But I wanted to make it clear, that this thing between us... it is no one else's business but yours and mine. And it is up to us what we want to do about it."

My heart was light as he drew my hand up and pressed a kiss onto it.

How could I have doubted him? How could I have doubted this?

"Mom would've loved you, by the way." Ronan ran his thumb over the backs of my fingers, his eyes soft.

I allowed myself to smile up at him. The heaviness weighing down my insides was gone. "Seems like you were born into the perfect family."

Ronan's smile seemed to freeze on his face.

Then the moment passed, and I was left wondering if I had imagined it altogether.

I mentally shrugged, and snuggled further into his solid chest.

It's been a long day. Stop being paranoid.

Everything is perfect... All you have to do is not screw it up.

CHAPTER 10

KARA

Ronan and I sat on the couch for a while longer, talking quietly about nothing in particular. My head rested on his chest, and I pressed into the warmth of his shirt, listening to the slow, steady beat of his heart.

The knot of anxiety in my chest began to ease.

I was used to keeping my own company. I didn't mind it most of the time; sometimes I even appreciated the solitude and drew strength from it. I'd convinced myself that my creative passions were enough, and that I was content to while away my days in the pack, watching other people be happy.

Meeting Ronan had changed all that.

For the first time, I allowed myself to imagine what it would be like: to stay here, in the Thornwood pack. A day ago, the idea would have filled me with horror.

But now...

Once the thought materialized in my head, I couldn't stop thinking about staying here, with Ronan. I kept mulling the idea over as we moved from the living room to the kitchen, where Ronan threw together a simple but delicious stir-fry after refusing to let me help with anything.

"You're still our guest, Kara!" he said, then dug out place settings for two.

With Kit still gone, it felt a little bit like, well, a date.

"I should've dressed fancier," I joked, as Ronan sat down opposite me.

He'd found a candlestick in the back of one of the cupboards and set it in a holder in the center of the table. It was a little bent out of shape—it clearly hadn't been used in years—and in the glow of the candlelight I caught him making a face.

"You don't need to dress up. You're gorgeous all the time." He picked up his fork and played with it absently, gazing at me with obvious interest. I managed to meet his eyes. I was getting better and better at accepting the attention instead of shying away from it.

"Thank you," I managed, though part of me didn't believe him. No one had ever shown me this level of interest, or if they had, I had never picked up on it. With Ronan, everything was different in that sense. New and undeniably exciting.

"All that other stuff is just... surface level. It's *you* that I want," he said.

"My inner soul?" I tilted my head at him, only half-joking.

He shot me a crooked grin. He didn't seem offended though, just... curious.

"Maybe." A spark entered his eyes. "The wolf in me wants the wolf in you."

"Is that all?"

Ronan stared at me for a long moment. I ached under his heated gaze. I pressed my thighs together under the table, wanting things I couldn't even put a name to.

"No, that's not all." *I want all of you.*

He didn't say that last bit out loud, but I could almost hear the words hovering there between us. I knew, because those words were on the tip of my tongue, too.

I grasped about for a new conversational topic, something that wouldn't result in me crawling over the table and into his lap right then and there.

"When I got here, I thought this place was so different from home." I clenched my fork. My mouth suddenly felt dry. I lifted my glass and took a sip of the wine before continuing, letting its sweetness flood over my tongue. "The people, the watchtowers... everything. But now I'm not so sure."

"What do you mean?"

I gestured around us, and Ronan looked around the kitchen, frowning.

"I'm not sure I follow."

I let out a soft sigh. "I *know* this house, Ronan. These walls. I've lived inside them too, at least metaphorically. Ever since I lost my parents."

My voice was gentle, but there was an undercurrent of sadness in it that I couldn't hide. No matter how long it had been, I knew the sadness would never go away. Not completely.

"For the longest time, my brother Jason and I were on our own. We had the pack, sure, but..." I bit my lip. "There were times when it felt like all we had was each other. The house we grew up in, our parents' house, became a memorial to them. It wasn't a place to live any more... just a reminder of everything we'd lost."

I gazed around at the kitchen. Like the rest of the house, the walls in here were bare of decoration.

"I'm sorry," Ronan murmured.

I reached out and grabbed his hand over the table. "I'm just saying... I get it."

"What changed?"

A smile blossomed across my face. "Jason found his mate. Tammy. A human girl, of all things."

Ronan's eyebrows shot up. "Wow."

"I know." My smile faded as I thought of them in that house, happy with the new life they'd just brought into the world. Making new memories to fill the space with love once again. "I'm happy for him."

"But...?"

I tilted my head, confused. "There's no *but*. All I want is for the people I love to be happy."

A wrinkle appeared between Ronan's eyebrows. "Of course. But you deserve happiness too, Kara. You deserve to make your own memories."

"I'm happy enough," I countered.

"I beg to differ."

I wanted to put an end to this conversation that had suddenly taken a ridiculous turn. We were debating my happiness, for some reason, when I was the happiest I'd ever been, sitting across from Ronan with nothing but a beat-up old candlestick between us.

I opened my mouth to say something to that effect, but before I could get any more words out, Ronan stood up and circled the table, hoisting me up out of my chair.

I gasped and flung my arms around his neck to steady myself. I wanted to protest. I could walk on my own two feet, thank you very much. Before I could say anything, he pressed his mouth against mine, hot and demanding.

It was exactly what I'd imagined doing to him, only a few minutes earlier, and now that he'd taken the initiative, I melted into the embrace.

I moaned as his arms tightened around my body, reveling in our closeness. When he pulled away, his gaze was determined behind the heat in his expression.

"You deserve everything," he growled. *"Everything."*

Well, when he put it that way... "I *want* everything," I whispered, and I had never spoken a truer word. I pulled his face down to mine, and we kissed with an intensity that left me trembling and weak on the inside.

In a move that left me dizzy, he lifted me up, encouraging my legs to wrap around his waist, and then he carried me upstairs. This time, he wasn't as controlled about it. Judging by the way he kept pausing to press hot-mouthed kisses over every inch of my skin he could reach, he was struggling to contain his desire. I shivered as I realized he was holding himself back from just taking me right there, in the hallway or on the stairs.

I wouldn't have cared at all. I was shameless, wanton. I needed to *feel* him, against me, around me and *inside* me, more than I had ever needed anything in my life.

I slid my hands up his back, clenching my thighs tighter around his waist and feeling his muscles shifting underneath his shirt. Once we reached the landing, he placed me down. I stumbled onto my tiptoes, arching up into his form, pressing the length of my body against his. My hands fisted into his shirt as I dragged him backwards toward the door of his bedroom.

I wanted him to be in no doubt at all, that this is what I wanted. Him, right here and right now.

My heart beat like a trapped bird inside my chest. I was dizzy with arousal, helpless to control the ache deep within me.

The night was only going to end one way.

I need to feel him inside me.

We made our way through the threshold of the room, and he backed me toward the bed without breaking his stride. There was none of last night's cautious restraint; he wasn't holding back anymore as he pressed down on top of me. The mattress sagged down under our combined weight, and I shifted and writhed up against him, giving as good as I got.

He pulled away from my mouth to look down at me. There was a wildness in his face; his hips thrust into mine, like he was unaware of the action. His tangled hair fell over his face, and in the half-darkness, there was no mistaking the wolf in him.

Good. I want it—I want it all.

He growled as my legs fell open around his hips, and my mouth parted in a wordless invitation. He leaned down over me and seared a kiss against my neck, tasting my fluttering pulse.

"No-one has touched you," he murmured, "before me?"

"No-one," I gasped.

He slid his fingers down and teased over the waistband of my jeans, and I bit back a needy moan.

"Only you."

His clever fingers worked open the zipper and brushed down, skirting the edge of my pussy until he had me panting with frustration. Before long, we both grew impatient, tired of the teasing. I worked off my jeans and fiddled with the buttons of my shirt, but Ronan had had enough. The fabric came apart between his fists, and shreds of fabric littered the bed around us. My bra soon followed, and before long I was naked beneath his hot, heaving chest and wild eyes.

Last night, Ronan had been the picture of control. He hadn't seemed worried for his own pleasure; he'd been content to drive me to orgasm and retreat downstairs for the rest of the night.

This was different.

This time, we were in it together: that crazed hunger that overcame all shifters when they found their true mate.

I squirmed a hand free and pawed at his t-shirt. He tugged it off, getting the message. My hands roamed over his chest as he stared down at me. When my hands made for his jeans, his fingers encircled my wrists and pushed me back down.

I wanted to cry out. To beg and plead, if I had to.

In the state I was in, I would do or say just about anything to get him to touch me.

"You've never been taken like this before." Ronan's voice rumbled through my own chest. "Have you?"

"Never." The word was almost wrenched out of me. "Please, I need you. I can't—"

My hips bucked up into his. I was so wet, and I would have been shame-faced if not for the feel of Ronan's hard cock pushing against the inside of his jeans. In spite of my impatient movements, he seemed unsure. His eyes flicked over my face, searching for something.

"What is it? I want you, Ronan. I need you. Don't stop."

Evidently, my permission must have been what he was looking for. My words galvanized him into action. His hands sprang from my wrists and he jumped up to drag off his clothing and free his erection before rejoining me on the bed. We both groaned as he shifted forward, and the head of his cock brushed over my clit.

"Ronan." I squirmed as he bore down against me, his mouth pressing into my neck, teeth and tongue working over my heated skin. "Please."

When he finally slid inside me, I was so wet and ready that there was only minimal resistance. He paused, then thrust a little harder, and the virginal barrier was gone. He filled me, the heat and intensity of being possessed like this almost too much to bear. I spread my legs as wide as I could, shameless in my need, and arched up into him.

He put his hands around my waist and pulled me into him. Then one of his hands found its way to the side of my head, fingers tangling in my hair. I buried my face in his heated neck, and he began to thrust into me.

He drew back and forced me to look at him. I wanted to blush, to duck away, but I couldn't escape his eyes.

Those damned eyes. After tonight, I'd never be able to look into them the same way again.

"Mine," he said. "You're mine, Kara. Mine to claim."

"Yours," I managed to gasp out.

In that moment, I knew it was true. Body and soul, he had me.

His thrusts were slow at first, testing, making allowance for this being my first time, but when my moans and gasps proved I was enjoying this as much as him, he picked up the pace and started driving into me in a steady, unrelenting rhythm. I was spread-eagled against the mattress, pinned in place with the force of his possession, helpless in the face of my mounting orgasm.

It crashed over me, wave after wave of pleasure coursing through my body as Ronan fucked me through it. I sobbed, loving the feeling of him surrounding me on all sides. One of his hands came down to rub my clit and I wanted to pull away—it was too much, too intense —but there was nowhere to go. I could only buck into his touch as he changed his angle slightly, and with another deep thrust, a second orgasm rolled through me.

After what felt like an endless sea of pleasure, Ronan buried himself deep and spilled into me with a groan. He tugged my head back, and he laid an open-mouthed kiss against my lips. I swallowed the sound of his orgasmic cries, drinking him in as eagerly as my body rippled around his cock.

A shiver ran down my spine at a sudden realization.

We didn't use protection.

There was a possibility that he'd claimed me in more ways than one.

I ached as he slowly pulled out of me. He hadn't been overly rough as far as I could tell, but the unfamiliarity of the act left me exhausted, physically and emotionally. He slumped down next to me and gathered me into his arms, rolling me into his side and pressing a kiss against the back of my shoulder. I pressed back into him. We were lying in a tangle of hot, damp sheets and the remains of my shirt, but I didn't care.

The long day, with all its emotional highs and lows, had finally caught up with me.

Beside me, Ronan's breathing settled. He mumbled something into my hair as he drifted off to sleep, but I didn't catch it.

I lay still for a few minutes, trying to process what had just happened, unable to fight the huge smile that lifted my lips. Pretty soon, I followed him into sleep.

CHAPTER 11
RONAN

Now that Kara and I had laid all our cards on the table in relation to how we felt, a strange sort of peace settled over the house.

Over the days that followed, we fell into a routine. Each morning, I headed out to attend to my pack duties. On good days, this meant patrolling with Noah or Jake, and on bad days it meant sitting through a seemingly endless council meeting and listening to the Elders strategize about this or that.

Usually, I returned in time for lunch with Kara. Sometimes Kit joined us, or it would just be the two of us. After, we'd sit out on the porch people-watching, and Kara would tell me about her morning.

She had taken it upon herself to renovate the house. It started with, in her words, sprucing up the kitchen and living room, before unfolding into a full-on transformation. After the morning I came home to find her cursing at the wall and holding her wrist, I enlisted the help of some of the guys for the manual labor, and by the end of the week, the wall that divided the kitchen and dining room was mostly gone, replaced by a couple of rustic beams that opened up the space and somehow made it cozier at the same time.

I began to notice small things appearing. Colored cushions on the sofa one day, followed by a throw in a soft, loose knit the next. Things that I hadn't seen for years—an old wind chime, a rusty planter, a watering can—all rescued and restored, or else repurposed into something new.

At first, she would ask me if I liked each new thing.

I always said, truthfully, that I loved it.

After a while, she stopped asking.

People around town—some teasing, some sincere—began to point out the change in me. How there was a new purpose to the way I walked, a true Alpha's glint in my eye. Even Kit, who had always been a happy kid but full of excess energy, seemed calmer, no longer skittering around the house like he was full of nervous tension.

It was all down to the positive influence of Kara.

I couldn't believe how lucky I had been to meet her. One day, I would have to visit Allara at the Bane pack and let her know how grateful I was that she had sent Kara in her place.

The peace and happiness for all of us was new, and it was welcome. But in my experience, good things didn't last.

I woke up in the night to the sound of movement coming from outside my bedroom window. I stirred, half-awake. Kara lay beside me, still deeply asleep, her hair spread out on the pillow and one of her hands curled up against her cheek. She looked adorable, and my dick stirred immediately.

Until I realized what had woken me. At the sound of a distant shout, I sat bolt upright in bed, amorous thoughts on hold.

Silently, I climbed out of bed and moved over to the window. My shifter senses were on high alert. I could hear more shouting in the distance, and the thud of running feet on the street outside.

A sleepy voice came from the bed behind me.

"What's the matter, Ronan?"

I turned around. Kara was gazing at me and rubbing her eyes.

"What's going on?" she asked.

"I don't know." Trepidation filled me. It sounded like some kind of attack. I glanced back outside, but it was too dark to see anything clearly, even with my shifter-enhanced vision. "Stay here, and lock the door behind me."

I quickly threw on some clothes and strode out of the room, taking the stairs two at a time. I slipped out of the house as silently as possible, praying that Kit was still asleep upstairs. He was too young to become involved in a battle, if this truly was an attack of some kind on our pack.

It was pitch dark outside. The rest of the houses were still and quiet. Whatever was happening, most of the pack still seemed to be oblivious.

I followed the sound of voices, my heart thudding under my shirt. I couldn't shake the feeling that something wasn't right, but I couldn't put my finger on what.

Then it hit me. Everything was dark, but it shouldn't be.

The lights from the watchtowers, those familiar beacons that shone over the town every night, were gone.

Thud.

I tensed up as I smacked into something warm and solid, and my hackles rose, instincts telling me to fight. A low growl slipped out of me.

"Ronan?"

At the sound of Jake's voice, I relaxed a touch.

"What's happening?" I asked. "An attack?"

My pack is in danger. The thought thrummed through my whole body. *I have to protect them. I have to protect Kara.*

"I don't know." The seriousness in Jake's usually carefree voice sent a chill down my spine. "I woke up and heard noises. Figured I'd come and find you."

I blinked, touched by his loyalty.

"Come on. This way." I tapped his shoulder, indicating that I wanted him to follow me.

Together, we crept through town, sticking to the sides of buildings to orient ourselves. Even with our shifter eyesight, it was nearly impossible to see much in the darkness.

Jake and I had been packmates all our lives, friends for years, and had done many guard duty hours together. We didn't need words as we soundlessly worked our way through town.

As we neared the edge of the square, we ran into Noah and Zac, who were crouched behind a high fence. A fire burned nearby and a spark of relief flooded me when their faces came into view, despite their grave expressions.

"The gates are open," Noah said. "Ronan, I think it's a coup. There's a group of people—shifters I'd say—and they said they're looking for you. And when they find you…"

My blood froze. I sprang to my feet. "I left Kit and Kara back at the house. I have to go back for them—"

Zac yanked me down again, ignoring the growl I sent his way. "No way. If you go back to that house now, you're a dead man."

"I don't care."

I wasn't thinking logically. I wasn't thinking at all.

"You may not care, but we do," Noah interjected. "We need a living Alpha, Ronan. Not a dead one."

"I'm no-one's Alpha," I hissed, forgetting that I'd started to slide automatically into the role over the past couple of weeks. Right now,

I didn't want to lead a pack. All I cared about was the safety of my younger brother, and the woman I—

"Guys, we can debate this later." Jake peered over the fence. I realized that the area beyond our hiding place was brighter, like more fires had been lit nearby. "We have to leave now, before they see us."

As we skirted around the edge of the square, I caught sight of a few of the figures gathered in the center, holding torches.

A woman's long hair shone in the firelight. As she turned her head, I got a good look at her.

Naomi.

A man I didn't recognize slid up alongside her and wrapped an arm around her waist. Her lips thinned, but she didn't push him away. He whispered something in her ear and a smile stretched across her face.

Something about that smile chilled me to the bone.

Enough of this. I wasn't born to crouch in the shadows, or slink away like some coward.

I turned to Jake and Zac. "Circle back to the front gates. Then close them. Cut these other shifters off from escape, make sure no-one else gets in."

I used my commanding tone, knowing they couldn't refuse. They turned away without a word and vanished into the night. I trusted them completely to get the job done.

I turned back to the clearing, my eyes narrowed as I considered and discarded options. In the end, there was only one option that made sense.

"Wait." Noah hovered at my shoulder. "I know that look. Ronan, this is a bad idea."

"I know," I muttered. "But it's the only idea I have."

It's me they want. Nobody else has to get hurt.

With a deep breath, I straightened upright and swaggered into the clearing.

CHAPTER 12
KARA

The minute Ronan ordered me to stay put, my hackles rose with fear mixed with a healthy dose of anger.

There's no way I'm staying here!

I wanted to yell after him as he swept out of the room, but the words stuck in my throat. Furious, I flung back the covers and stumbled into the clothes that had been abandoned by the side of the bed earlier that night.

I remembered the way Ronan had torn them off me, frenzied with passion.

I squeezed my eyes tight shut, and drew a deep breath.

Now is the time to be brave.

Without thinking twice, I pulled on my clothes and headed for the door.

The landing was dark. As I crossed over it toward the stairs, the door cracked open behind me and a chink of light appeared, along with Kit's sleep-tousled hair.

"Kara?" His voice was rough and gritty with sleep. "I heard something."

I glanced back at him. "I know. I'm going outside. Stay here, okay?"

"Where's Ronan?"

I paused, one foot hovering over the top step.

I couldn't lie to him. Ronan was his brother—he deserved the truth. It was what I would've wanted in his position. "He left already."

We exchanged a long look. With each minute that ticked past, I was more awake, more alert. The silence prickled against my eardrums.

Something was wrong.

Kit slid out of his room, flannel PJs and all, and shut the door behind him. Even in half-shadow, I could see the determination on his face. "I'm coming with you."

"No, Kit—"

"If you try to tell me it's too dangerous..." His eyes flashed at me, and I caught a hint of his shifter beneath the surface. Young, feral. Ready for action. "Save it, okay? He's my *brother*. I know you understand."

I nodded. I understood all too well. I had just been angry with Ronan, because he had assumed I was too weak to help, and demanded I stay put. It would be hypocritical of me if I did exactly the same thing to Kit now.

"Be careful, okay. Ronan loves you so much, Kit..."

"I know. That's why I need to help."

After a moment I nodded. There wasn't time to argue. We headed downstairs together, slipping on the first pairs of shoes we could find in the darkened hallway, and snuck out into the night.

The streets were mostly empty, but there were a handful of other people from the pack who had heard the noise and come out like us to see what was going on. We found ourselves in the middle of a group of people who were heading toward the town square. It seemed to be where the action was, with the flicker of flames in that direction drawing us all like the proverbial moths.

By the time we made it to the edge of the clearing, the crowd was thick enough that we had to nudge our way through to the front.

My heart plummeted down to earth and I had to clench my hands into fists to stop them trembling.

Ronan stood alone at the center of the clearing. He was surrounded on all sides by shifters. They didn't seem to be from this pack. Even though I didn't know everyone here on a personal level yet, I'd seen a lot of Ronan's pack around the village since I'd been here and at least knew them to look at. These shifters were strangers, stony-faced and threatening.. Some of them were in wolf form, and they padded around the edge of the square like moving shadows. Circling Ronan, as if he were prey.

One of the strangers stepped forward into the light, and my heart all but stopped.

He wasn't a stranger, not to me.

Jaime.

He looked unchanged from the last time I'd seen him, when he'd turned up to fight Allara, assuming he was going to kill her and win the Alpha spot. Same smug, smirking face, same sandy hair. Only a deep scar, bisecting his left eyebrow and carving an ugly crevice down his cheek, spoke of his fight for dominance against Allara all those months ago.

A smaller figure slunk up beside him. *Naomi?* Was she with Jaime, now? A sick feeling settled in my gut. Individually, Jaime and Naomi were poison. Together, they would likely be deadly.

The two of them moved forward like some twisted parody of an Alpha pair, coming to a standstill about five feet away from Ronan.

He wasn't moving. The only indication of the emotion I knew must be bubbling inside him were his clenched fists. Even from here, I could see his white-knuckled grip.

"I guess we have an audience now," Jaime said, his voice ringing out through the clearing. "It looks like this takeover won't be as peaceful as I hoped."

Ronan's face twisted. "You mean you can't kill me in my sleep, now that the pack is here to bear witness?" He swept out a hand toward Jaime and whirled around. "Behold, your would-be Alpha, everyone. A coward who attacks under the cover of darkness, because he knows he'd never win in a fair fight. The Bane pack's Alpha proved that, already."

The smile on Jaime's face instantly disappeared. His eyes glittered coldly. "At least I know what I am. What I *can* be. You had all the power at your fingertips, there for the taking, and you ran away. What sort of Alpha runs away and leaves his pack unprotected? Why do you think I'm here? There's a power vacuum, Ronan." He shrugged. "You didn't step up."

"You will never be Alpha of this pack," Ronan said. His voice rang out clearly, strong and sure. The flames burning around the clearing flickered, and several people gasped. "Get out of here, before I tear you apart."

Jaime's smile reappeared. "The truth is," he said, obviously playing to his captive audience and making sure we all caught every word, "deep down, you know you aren't the man for the job. Everyone knows it."

His eyes narrowed, and his voice dropped into a hiss. "Your *father* knew it."

Ronan let out a growl so powerful, I felt it rumble through the ground beneath my feet. Everyone around me held their breaths. Even Naomi took a small, involuntary step back. Jaime looked surprised, but he held his ground.

A mist was churning up in the center of the clearing. Dust rose from the ground, and static flashed in the air.

Ronan was shifting.

Jaime's eyes flashed with something. I couldn't tell if it was panic or anger. But he damn sure hadn't expected to have to fight Ronan. The coward had planned to kill Ronan in his sleep.

He didn't have any choice, now. Jaime crouched low in the dirt, a cloud of mist rising up around him to mirror Ronan's own.

The wolves patrolling around the edge of the square threw back their heads and howled.

My chest grew tight, and my gut churned. I felt it: that familiar urge, the instinct to let the wild creature inside me run free. It was the strongest call I'd had in years. Stronger than my first, uncontrolled shifts, stronger even than the first time I'd laid eyes on Ronan and realized he was my fated mate.

I bit my lip so hard I tasted blood. Now wasn't the time to lose control.

Beside me, Kit shifted his weight from one foot to the other, as if he were fighting against the same urge as me.

Unable to drag my eyes away from Ronan, I reached out blindly and grabbed at Kit's wrist, shaking my head.

Don't do it, Kit. Control yourself.

Young shifters couldn't always help it when they shifted sometimes—especially when they were scared, or angry. The skill only became more controlled with time and experience.

Inside the clearing, Ronan drew himself up to his full height. He was a massive wolf. His russet fur gleamed in the firelight, and his thick pelt rippled across his broad, bulky frame. Despite Jaime's taunts, his features were unmistakably those of an Alpha's bloodline and it was strikingly apparent to everyone there that they were looking at an Alpha wolf.

He shook himself off in a familiar motion, and his head dropped low, eyes narrowed and deadly as he readied himself to fight.

Poised to strike, he stood taller than Jaime in wolf form, and every muscle in his body tensed. One-on-one, he was in a good posi-tion to defeat the rogue intruder. But he was outnumbered. Already the other wolves were crowding in, ready to defend Jaime at a second's notice.

The back of my neck prickled, and my mouth went dry.

Unconsciously, one of my hands came up to rest over my abdomen.

Jaime's ears flicked, and he glanced at the wolf to his left side. The wolf slunk backwards, and the others followed.

Okay. So this isn't a pile-on. Not yet, anyway.

This is a fight for control of the Thornwood pack.

Something in the air shifted. Ronan's muzzle came up and his eyes slid past Jaime—and landed on me.

I poured everything I felt for Ronan into my expression, praying it would give him strength.

Then Jaime lunged at Ronan.

I jumped, my heart pounding as I watched the man who should be my mate, handle an attack from a man I knew to be vicious and unhinged.

There wasn't going to be any mercy here tonight. This would be a fight to the death.

Both were going in for the kill.

Ronan twisted away from Jaime, then lunged in, his jaws latching onto the back of Jaime's neck; he lifted him into the air and shook him before slamming him back down to earth. Jaime snarled and shook himself free, slinking backwards, his belly against the earth.

I was fixated on the fight. I didn't even blink.

I sent out a soundless, desperate prayer into the darkness.

Please, Ronan, you have to finish this.

For me. For us.

I was barely conscious of who I meant. Us—the pack? Me and Kit? Or something else? Something that I was too elated and afraid to even name. Perhaps it was for the tiny something that could be growing inside me right now as I watched the man I loved fight for his life.

Sharp, vicious snarls and growls pierced the air, and I snapped back into the present.

Naomi had joined the fray and advanced while Ronan's back was turned. She was sleeker than Jaime, with fur that shone white in the shadows.

Ronan's ear flicked outwards as she grew closer. He knew she was there, but he was too busy fending off Jaime's snapping jaws to do anything about her.

Then I realized that my hand, the one that had been locked on Kit's wrist, was empty.

Shit.

Russet fur flashed at the edge of the clearing. My heart thundered in my chest and adrenalin zinged along my veins. Kit was in wolf form and advancing around the circle, keeping to the shadows but obviously trying to position himself to launch into defense of his brother.

Several of Jaime's wolves turned to Kit.

My mouth formed a single, soundless word. *No!*

As if we were psychically connected and he'd heard me, Ronan's head snapped up. He immediately saw what was about to happen, and charged Jaime, tossing him to one side. He bounded past Naomi like she wasn't even there. His eyes were wide with fear, and fixed on his brother.

He was too far away. Jaime's wolves sprang on Kit and dragged him down in a blur of teeth and fur and snarls. Kit whined and tried to lash out, but the wolves were too big to fight, too strong to throw off, and too many to defeat.

Ronan skidded to a halt in front of Kit's fallen form and let out a snarl so powerful it was almost a roar. He grabbed the nearest wolf in his jaws and tore him away, sending him tumbling to the ground in a mess of blood and fur. Another of Kit's attackers snapped at him, but he twisted aside and then lunged for him, knocking the wolf aside and slashing out with his huge paws.

Kit lay on the ground, curled onto one side. From this angle, I couldn't see if he was still breathing.

My vision blurred. My heart thundered in my chest.

I couldn't control my shifter any longer. My family needed saving.

I dropped to my knees and the world around me dissolved. When I blinked and straightened up, I wasn't fully Kara anymore. My shifter was in the driver's seat.

For once, I didn't try to suppress my wolf instincts. I simply got out of its way and let it take control.

I crept forward.

Being a wolf again was surreal. It had been months, maybe even a year, since I'd been in this form. Every blade of grass under my feet, every brush of wind on my face, every subtle movement of the crowd surrounding the square flooded my senses.

I couldn't get distracted.

Ronan was caught up with Jaime again. Naomi was watching them, waiting for a chance to jump in and help Jaime. She hadn't noticed me. I had the element of surprise.

I bounded forward and lunged at her, sinking my jaws into her neck without hesitation.

I'd never attacked anyone like this in my life.

It felt surprisingly good, given the recipient was Naomi.

My human mind, buried deep under thick layers of shifter instinct and rage, replayed every encounter with her over the years. The sly comments, the casual cruelty. The way she'd tossed Jason aside when it was convenient, then came running back the second he found someone better. Her shameless greed, her ambition for power.

And now, her desire to destroy Ronan. I could not forgive, nor let that slide.

Not anymore.

She managed to roll me over, dislodging me off her neck, but I had drawn blood, and I wanted more. She snarled in my face, long teeth glistening. I arched up and growled straight back at her, baring my lips to reveal my own shifter teeth.

It was obvious she was the more experienced fighter of the two of us. But I had something she didn't have: unstoppable anger, and the drive to protect my family.

With a sharp twist, I pounced and pinned her to the ground, my front paws on her neck and chest. Her white fur, so flawless before, was marred and tangled. I probably looked similar, but I didn't care.

A crack rang out like a gunshot over the square.

I jerked up my head, looking for Ronan, and felt the jolt of shock through Naomi's body beneath my paws as she arched her head in the same direction as me.

Jaime lay at Ronan's feet, still and lifeless.

Cold shock rushed over me. A couple of whining noises from the edge of the clearing caught my attention. The wolves from Jaime's pack were crowded together, pinned down by three newcomers that I suspected were Noah, Zac, and Jake.

A small, pained sound came from a few feet away.

Kit.

Like a spell had been broken, I climbed off Naomi and left her on the ground, walking away from her toward Kit. She didn't try to get up.

Ronan was already standing over Kit when I got there, nudging at him with his muzzle. He looked up as I approached but allowed me to press up against his side. Another shifter approached, but Ronan snarled at him until he backed away.

Kit's chest was rising and falling in short, shallow breaths. Ronan nudged him again and whined, a low, awful sound that set my fur on edge.

I couldn't imagine this village without Kit's smiling, happy face in it, and I'd only known him a short time. Ronan must have been so scared at the thought of losing his only sibling.

Out of the corner of my eye, I caught movement.

The crowd parted to let someone through. Elder Frey strode into the middle of the clearing and spread his arms out wide.

"The challenger has been killed," he said. Even from this distance, I could see his expression, grave and stone-like. "Go home, all of you."

Something flickered in my chest. Doubt, maybe. Or confusion.

Why wasn't he declaring Ronan the victor?

I shook my head and refocused on Kit, who was just beginning to stir. I'd held a grudge against the Elder ever since he'd taken me aside and told me Ronan wasn't cut out to be a mate.

Ronan is the perfect mate. For me.

I stared again at Elder Frey, whose lips were tight as he glared around at the crowd.

It's probably nothing.

We had far bigger problems right now.

CHAPTER 13
RONAN

The next few days passed in a blur.

I couldn't keep track as days faded into nights. I sat beside Kit's bed, the changing light outside the window my only source of company.

Kara brought me food occasionally, slipping in and out of the room and closing the door softly behind her. I must have eaten, but I barely registered what passed my lips. Sometimes she sat with me, and together we shared the silence that lay like a thick fog over everything.

I couldn't even begin to face the thought of life without my brother by my side.

On the third day, Kit woke up.

I was dozing face down on the bedspread when I felt a soft poke against the top of my head. I jolted, mumbling and blinking the sleep out of my eyes.

"Kara?" I muttered.

"No." The voice was scratchy with disuse, but it made my heart sing. "Your brother."

My eyes opened properly and I sat up so fast I felt dizzy. Kit was resting against his pillow. He was still pale, but he was awake. And smiling at me.

"Hey." I poured him a glass of water from the bedside table and handed it over. He drained it in one swallow, then wiped a hand over his face. "How do you feel?"

"Like I got run over by a truck." Kit ran a hand through his mussed hair and cocked his head to the side. "What happened?"

"What do you remember?"

"Not much." Kit struggled to sit up, shuffling around and ignoring my hand on his shoulder, trying to get him to lie still. "I remember the fight. Those other wolves getting ready to attack you. I thought I might be able to distract them... help you... But after that, it's all a blur."

"The coup failed. Jaime's dead. It's over."

Kit raised an eyebrow.

"You killed him."

He said it as a statement rather than a question, like he had every confidence in me.

I nodded slowly. "I did. But it was close."

"Are you okay, Ronan? And Kara?"

"We are. The storm has passed, I swear, Kit. We're safe."

Kit grinned. "You beat the challenger. Congrats."

I didn't smile back.

When I thought of the life I had taken, mixed emotions rose in my chest. Bitterness, sorrow... and the sure-fire certainty that I would do it all again if I had to.

I'd do anything to keep the ones I loved safe.

But I wasn't ready for Kit to learn about the guilt that came with killing a man, yet. To see the look in his eyes when he learned the truth. Killing didn't bring triumph. Killing was a last resort and always something that weighed heavily on a person's soul, even if the death was deserved, or in self-defense.

"Does this mean you've accepted, then?"

I blinked, snapping back to the present. "What?"

"That you're our Alpha," Kit said carefully, like I was slow on the uptake. "The ceremony doesn't have to be a huge deal, Ronan. It's just a formality, right?"

I said nothing, plucking at a loose thread in the duvet cover.

Luckily, Kit's attention had already wandered to other things. Now that he was awake, that restless teenage energy was back with a vengeance. He moved under the covers, as if about to get up, and I shook my head, pushing him back down.

"No way, man. You're still healing."

"Ronan." Kit's voice had gone full little-brother-whine. His eyes widened as I climbed to my feet and headed toward the door. "C'mon, I'm *fine*."

"Even shifters need time to recover." I remained firm, even when Kit rolled his eyes and slumped back down again. "Give your body a chance to heal, okay? At least until tomorrow."

As I left the room, I hoped the palpable relief in my voice wasn't as obvious to my brother as it was to me.

Three days ago, we weren't sure he was going to wake up at all.

I stood outside his door, and gave an involuntary sigh of relief. Soaking in the reality of the fact that my brother was alive and going to be okay.

I didn't have a chance to bask in the relief for long. Already, the respite was draining away. I had other problems, and now there was nothing to distract from them.

Like an echo, his words filtered through from the back of my mind.

You're our Alpha.

My ribcage felt several sizes too tight. I tried to draw in a deep breath, but my lungs were being squeezed inwards.

Fresh air. That's what I need.

My heart hammered as I jogged down the staircase. I hadn't so much as set foot outside in days. A good run through the forest would clear my airways and soothe the tension thrumming along the length of my spine.

Kara came out of the kitchen. Seeing the look on my face, she buried herself in my arms. "He's awake?"

"He is." I pressed my face against the top of her head, comforted. "Thank you," I mumbled, pulling away to kiss her properly. "For everything."

Her eyes shone up at me, and I cupped a hand against her cheek, tucking a few loose strands of hair behind her ear.

"I've got a surprise for you." Her smile was soft. "Look... just here."

She led me away from the foot of the stairs, across the hall to the wall on the other side.

I came to a standstill.

The wall, which had been bare for almost a year now, had been transformed.

The photos from the file I kept buried in my closet—the same ones I'd shown Kara, all those weeks ago—had been arranged in a pretty collage on the wall. I didn't recognize the eclectic bundle of frames that housed the pictures: they were mismatched, but they all somehow fit together.

Some pictures were of Kit and me, down by the creek, arms slung around each other's shoulders with matching smiles. Noah, Jake and Zac were holding beers in one of the photos, while my teenage self frowned from the corner of the frame. There was even a recent one of me and Kara, in the garden behind the house, standing amongst the sunflowers. I think Kit took that one, a couple of weeks ago.

Dad was everywhere. Standing center stage in the meeting

house, swinging Kit in his arms, laughing and clapping a man on the shoulder. I leaned closer, realizing the other man was Elder Frey, just a less grizzled version than the one I knew.

In the central frame, my mom and dad stared out at me. I was perched on Dad's shoulders with a wide, cheery grin; in Mom's arms, baby Kit was sleeping peacefully.

I tried to speak, but when I opened my mouth, nothing came out.

All the tiredness, rage, confusion and frustration that had been building up over the days I'd spent at Kit's bedside rushed over me. I swayed backwards on my feet, unable to take my eyes off the picture in the middle.

From my father's unyielding, frozen gaze.

You're our Alpha.

Kara put her hand on my arm. "What do you think? Do you like it?"

～

*K*ARA

With each passing moment, each second of silence that dragged out, my anxiety grew.

I thought he'd love the collection of photos. I'd spent ages picking through them all to find ones that resonated with who I believed Ronan to be. I wanted to give him this reminder of all the relationships he valued; everyone who had cared for and supported him over the years.

Ronan stared at the collage with an unreadable expression. He was so still, he could've been a statue. Only the slow rise and fall of his chest told me otherwise.

I glanced again at the wall, my stomach sinking.

I'd wanted to channel all the nervous energy I'd built up over the past week into something productive. Something that would brighten up the barren hallway. Something that could remind Ronan what he had right in front of him.

The life he had, the people he'd loved. Even those he'd lost.

I thought it would help him come to terms with what had happened.

Now, doubt flooded through me. Had I overstepped the mark?

Ronan seemed to appreciate all the other little changes I'd made around the place. Maybe I'd gotten carried away, this time.

Finally, Ronan's shoulders hunched forward, and he turned away. His eyes dragged past mine without meeting them on his way over to the door. He opened it, then paused with his hand on the door handle.

"The kid's restless already," he said. "You should go see him."

I glanced back toward the photos on the wall. With the light of the sunset flooding in from the porch, the glass of the frames glimmered.

Ronan's eyes were fixed on the floor. He couldn't seem to look at either the photos, or me any longer.

"I will." I was proud of myself for holding my voice steady. "But only once you've told me what's wrong."

"I'm fine," he shot back, his eyes hard.

It wasn't an expression I was used to getting from him. All that affection and warmth seemed to have vanished. This was not the Ronan I knew.

He moved to close the door, but I swept forward before I knew what I was doing and pushed my way through, following him outside.

"No," I said. "You're not. Ronan, I'm sorry. I wanted it to be a surprise. I thought it would cheer you up."

"It's fine." He dragged a hand over his face. "Kara, I just need some air. I need to take a walk."

Stupid and irrational as it was, a surge of crushing panic swept over me.

The part of me that was human—the rational, level-headed part —knew the panic was ridiculous. But I couldn't help it. The other part was terrified of losing its mate. It wouldn't listen to reason. The fear was primal, lodged deep in my chest.

The worst part was, I couldn't fight it.

He got halfway down the steps before I put a hand on his shoulder. "Ronan. Please. Just *talk* to me."

Stay. The word hovered in the air between us, unspoken.

Under my hand, his body stiffened. He turned his head to the side so that I could see his darkened profile. "I'm done with talking right now."

"Well, I'm not! You've been watching over your brother for days, barely talking to anyone. And now you can't even *look* at me!"

The mention of his brother seemed to crack through the surface of whatever wall Ronan had put up. He wheeled around at me. "Because I've been trying to take care of the only family I have left!"

I bit down hard on my lip to quell the tears that threatened to spring up. My shifter was growing frustrated, and with frustration came anger.

My throat burned, and my breath came out fast and uneven. "And what are the rest of us meant to do? You're acting like you're alone, but you're *not*. My clan—"

Ronan's mouth curled bitterly. "Your clan? Your clan let Jaime go free. Your *reckless* Alpha almost got my brother killed."

"Don't you *dare* talk about Allara like that."

We were almost nose to nose, staring each other down without blinking. I hated how Ronan's sheer proximity always made my heart race in my chest. It was totally inappropriate, but heat coiled in my gut, and not entirely for the right reasons.

Ronan's gaze darted to my mouth. He huffed out a long breath. "I don't endanger me and mine, Kara."

"Neither does she." I looked up at him, and my breath caught at his burning gaze. "There's a difference between protecting people and holding them prisoner."

"What are you saying?"

"This place, these walls. You're not keeping people safe—you're locking them in. I have a brother too." The words were coming out fast, harsher than I intended, but I didn't care. "One I haven't seen in *weeks*. And a sister-in-law—and a niece."

I let out a short laugh that bordered on hysteria. "What am I even still *doing* here? If you would turn like this, so cold and unfeeling..."

Something flashed across Ronan's face. For a brief second, he looked anguished. "Kara."

"Maybe it's time for me to go back to my own family. My *clan*." My breath hitched as I held back a sob. "Now that Jaime's gone."

"Kara, *wait*."

I shook my head, darting out of his grasp as I descended the steps of the porch.

"That's why I'm here, right?" I whirled around toward his stricken face. "You needed collateral. Something to keep your truce with the Bane Clan. I was so stupid. I thought... well, it doesn't matter what I thought. I was wrong."

Ronan growled. He started after me, but I skittered out of reach.

"Don't be ridiculous," he shouted.

"Ridiculous? I'm being ridiculous?" The fire inside my heart was burning, and nothing could put it out. "Jaime's dead now. The clans are safe. There's no-one left to challenge you. You don't need me here anymore."

"Kara!" Ronan's voice resonated through my chest. From the way he was holding himself, I knew he was on the verge of shifting.

I didn't want that to happen, because I knew that, if he did, I would shift too.

I backed away slowly, shaking my head.

"Just..." Tears tracked down my cheeks, flowing freely. "Don't."

I couldn't look at him anymore. I turned and fled, ignoring his booming voice, and the sound of my name fading into the distance. Only one thought consumed me.

I have to get out of here. Away from him.

I MADE it to the edge of the village in one piece.

Nobody tried to stop me. Here and there, people gave me vague smiles, or raised a hand in greeting, but I hurried on. If my tear-stained face raised any eyebrows, I didn't stick around to find out.

Only one face stood out among the townsfolk I passed. Elder Frey stared at me as I hurried past the meeting house. He was in the upper window, standing in the same place I'd been when I first laid eyes on Ronan. His face was unreadable, not smiling or frowning, just... watchful.

A tremor ran down my spine, but I kept going.

As I reached the gates, I'd worked myself into a rage so powerful I was fully prepared to start kicking them down if they didn't open.

But they did. I didn't see who was manning the watchtowers, but I passed between the high fences for the first time since I'd arrived.

I didn't stop running until I was deep in the forest.

Only then did I allow myself to break down. I sobbed for what felt like hours, until I had no more tears left to cry. Until I trembled on my feet, light-headed and empty. I wanted to curl up on the forest floor and sleep. I wanted to sink down into the earth and just forget everything that had happened in the past few days.

Behind me, the foliage rustled. I inhaled sharply, pressing my back against a nearby tree, and held my breath.

A deer trotted out into the open. Relief flooded through me, so powerful that I almost laughed out loud.

I can't stay here. I'm too close to the Thornwood boundary. I have to get over to the other side of the creek.

I dug deep, feeling around for my shifter. It was curled up, burrowed away from the light. Slumbering. Heartbroken.

Tough shit. I needed my shifter now, in order to get home safely.

I couldn't travel like this. My frail human body couldn't trek through the forest, especially with my emotions torn to shreds. I needed my shifter's speed and agility.

After a few deep breaths, I finally felt my shifter stir. The change spread through me, starting at my feet, building in my chest. The wolf was here.

Time to go home.

CHAPTER 14

RONAN

For the longest time, I stood on the porch, gob-smacked that she had ignored my commanding tone.

I dismissed the thought of running after her. It was no use. I'd seen the look on her face before she turned away. Her mind was made up. We were both alike in that way. We made decisions and followed through on them.

Stubborn, a voice in the back of my mind whispered.

I snorted. Eventually, I slouched down onto the top step, staring out at nothing. I was in shock, the argument that had come out of nowhere still drumming through my head on a loop. I didn't know how it had escalated so quickly from one minute to the next.

I squeezed my eyes shut. Maybe when I opened them again, Kara would be back, and all the terrible things we'd said would be undone.

I opened my eyes.

I was alone.

A hopeless certainty filled me. Kara wasn't coming back. Even if I went to the Bane Clan, crawling on my hands and knees, that Reid guy, Allara's mate, would run me out of their territory on principle.

Fuck.

A floorboard creaked behind me, and I looked up to see Kit hobbling toward me.

"Thought I told you to stay in bed," I grumbled, although there wasn't much heat behind the words. "What happened to resting up?"

"I heard the angry voices." Kit dropped down beside me, like it wasn't weird to him that I was sitting out here on my own. "What's up? Where's Kara?"

"Gone."

Something in my tone of voice made Kit stare hard at me. I could feel his gaze, but I didn't turn and look at him, just frowned into the middle distance.

"What did you do?" His tone dripped with suspicion.

I was offended enough to look up. "What makes you think it was *me?*"

Kit just gave me a look. I slouched forward, resting my elbows on my knees.

"Told her the truth," I said. "I've got one job, as far as I can see. Since Dad died, I'm your only family, Kit. I have to look out for you."

"That's what you told her?"

I nodded. My chest felt hollow.

"You're an idiot."

My head snapped up. "What?"

If he wasn't still recovering, I would've put him in a headlock. *First my mate turns against me, now my brother?*

I was so indignant that it took me a second to realize I'd just thought of Kara as my *mate.*

"Do you really feel that way?" Kit gaped at me, outraged. "That it's just the two of us? That she's not *family?*"

"I—" He was right. I knew it deep down in my soul. Kara *was* family, and I had just watched her walk out of here on her own. I had let her down, just like I'd always done, with family. With obligation.

Kit dropped his head to his chest when he saw the look on my face. He scrubbed a hand through his hair, tousling it in every direction, then looked up again.

"Wait, is this about those pictures in the hallway? I saw them on my way out here." He wasn't indignant anymore. His voice had gone quiet. He sounded older than usual. His boyish expression was gone, replaced by something sober and deep with understanding.

For the first time, I realized that he was growing up.

I set my jaw and said nothing. I didn't need to. My silence said it all.

"I like them," Kit whispered eventually. "Especially the ones of Mom."

I still didn't trust myself to speak. I just nodded and dragged a hand over my mouth, wincing at the coarse stubble around my chin. I needed to shave.

"When you were little," I said eventually, my voice rough, "you broke your arm climbing in the forest."

"I know," Kit replied slowly. "I was there. Hurt like a bitch."

"I was meant to be watching over you." I turned to face him. "But Noah had found something. A cave near the mouth of the river. I lost track of you up in the canopy. You were like a spider-monkey."

I smiled at the memory.

Then, the smile faded. "I heard this *crack.* And you were bawling your head off. I carried you on my back, all the way home."

Kit snickered, shaking his head. "I don't remember any of *that.*"

"Dad was so mad," I continued. "He got right up in my face. I still remember his exact words. *You'll never make an Alpha like this, boy. Alphas watch out for their own. It's in your blood. Never forget that.*"

Kit, for once, was quiet.

"I failed you, Kit. I didn't keep you safe. And you almost died again a few days ago." I punched my hand hard into the side of the porch. "Because of me."

With slow, hesitant movements, Kit grabbed onto the stair rail and got to his feet.

"Bullshit. I wanted to fight. I'm grown, Ro. I can make my own choices." He jabbed a finger into my arm. "Stop using me as a distraction, and start thinking about how you're gonna win back the only woman you've ever truly cared about."

He began to limp toward the door, and I called out after him. I knew better than to offer a helping hand. I'd only land myself another poke, or worse.

"When did you get so perceptive?"

"Always have been." He shot me a sunny smile as he opened the door. Then his smile dropped, and he shot a glance inside, expression turning serious. "Want me to take those down?"

He jerked his head at the wall where the photos were hanging.

I shook my head. Kara had worked hard on that, for me. It was time I showed her my appreciation. And so much more. It was time to go get my mate back. If she'd have me.

I got to my feet, stretching out ligaments that were stiff with disuse. "You're right, Kit," I admitted. "I *am* stupid. And I gotta go fix things, before it's too late."

KARA

By the time I reached the road that led toward home, the sky had opened, and it was pouring with rain.

Droplets hammered down onto my back as I raced through the forest, sliding through my fur and turning the forest floor into a muddy quagmire. I dashed through wet leaves and slithered under low-hanging branches, relying on my shaky mental map of the area until I hit a familiar track.

My paws thundered on the ground, and I let the rhythm soothe my senses and lull me into a state nearing calmness.

I was going home.

Back to my life, the place I knew best. The only place, up until recently, I had ever been. Back to my family and friends, familiar rhythms and routines. Old, well-worn patterns.

My haven, where I could hide away from the world.

I came to a halt near the edge of my village, my heart crying out with relief. I'd made it. I was home.

A familiar figure trudged through the downpour carrying a bunch of sodden firewood on his back. If I'd been in human form I would have burst into tears at the sight of him, but instead I let out a low whine.

Reid.

He heard me and whirled, and the logs tumbled to the ground, forgotten.

I let out a soft bark in greeting and managed to stumble forward a couple of paces before exhaustion washed over me, and I fell to the ground at his feet. I was distantly aware of the thud of more footsteps rushing toward me, but I didn't have the energy to raise my head and see who it was.

The sound of my brother's voice, shouting something in alarm, was the last thing I registered before everything went black.

~

WHEN I WOKE UP, I was me again. Human, tucked up in my own bed, under a pile of soft woolen blankets.

Pale light drifted in from the window, and the long shadows across the floor told me it was late afternoon.

Groaning, I pulled the covers over my head and sank back into unconsciousness without another thought.

I woke up properly early the following morning.

I ached all over from yesterday's mad dash through the forest. Inside, my shifter was quiet again, still licking its wounds.

I curled onto my side and pressed my face against the pillow, willing myself to go back to sleep. I didn't want to be awake, and have to start thinking about what had happened with Ronan.

All I'd wanted was to come home. Now I was here: back in my own room, surrounded by familiar things. Paint pots littered the desk under the window, and a half-finished blanket lay over the back of the armchair in the corner.

My bedroom was like a time-capsule. A snapshot of my life on the day I'd left the pack with Reid. I hadn't expected everything to change that day. I hadn't realized that, when I did finally return, I would be vastly different to the innocent girl who had left.

More than anything, I wanted to go back to that day. To tell myself not to get in the truck, and not to leave pack territory.

But it was no use. There was no going back.

I dragged the pillow over my head and tried desperately to push down the tight feeling that squeezed my chest.

I can't believe I've been so stupid.

I'd actually begun to let myself believe that I could have... more. More than this room, this life.

I had thought that Ronan and I belonged together. That he saw me as *family*—someone worth protecting, someone to make new memories with after laying old ghosts to rest.

Now I saw how naïve I'd been. How childish.

Elder Frey had been right all along. Ronan didn't want or need a mate. He wasn't going to step up and become Alpha of his clan.

Nothing would change that, especially not a woman he'd only known for a few weeks.

The pillow grew damp under my face as tears leaked onto it.

I'll just stay in bed today. I'll deal with the fallout from all of this tomorrow.

I wasn't ready to show my face around the village just yet. I couldn't face the questions. The looks of confusion. Or worse, pity.

Would they all know—would they be able to tell—that I had met the person I thought would be my mate, and he had essentially rejected me?

I'd just begun to drift back into a light slumber when a sharp knock jolted me awake again.

"Go away," I called out. My voice was weak and scratchy. I slumped down, defeated, when the door opened anyway. "Jason, just go…"

I trailed off in surprise, blinking. Tammy shut the door behind her, then turned to face me with her hands on her hips.

"Oh," I said stupidly. "I thought you were my brother."

She leveled me with a look, then grabbed the chair from my desk and dragged it over to my bed before plopping herself down on it.

"I don't wanna talk," I said weakly.

"Yeah?" Tammy raised an eyebrow. "Well, I don't want to be awake at the ass-crack of dawn. But here we are."

I fell into a miserable silence, slumping back on my pillow. Her expression softened slightly as her eyes raked over my face.

Oh God, my hair is probably a bird's nest. Running through the forest, even though in wolf form, was not conducive to a good hair day the next morning.

"Allara put you to bed last night," Tammy said. "You were pretty out of it. She thinks this is all her fault. She's the reason you left in the first place."

"It's not her fault." I raked a hand over my face. Every movement was exhausting. "I just…I didn't belong there."

My throat was sore from holding back the misery.

"With the Thornwoods?"

I stared up at the ceiling. "I guess I don't really belong anywhere," I whispered. "Tammy, I can't go out there. I can't face it."

"Reid told me..." Tammy paused, like she wasn't sure she should continue. "You found your mate. The Thornwood heir. That's why you stayed."

I let out an empty laugh. So everyone *did* know. "Ronan and I... no-one will understand. Destiny, fated mates, what does it matter? We're from totally separate worlds."

She *snorted*.

At my shocked, affronted look, she just shook her head at me, folding her arms over her chest. We were roughly the same age, but suddenly, I felt like I was about to get told off.

"Nobody will understand?" Tammy scoffed. "Kara, I'm a *human* living in the middle of a wolf pack!"

"Tammy—" I managed to sit up properly, chagrined at the look on her face, but she wasn't finished.

"You think you're the only one who fell for someone they didn't expect?" Tammy's eyes flashed. She might not have been a shifter, but her strong will was more than a match for my own. "The only one who comes from a different world?"

I twisted my fingers in the bed sheets. "That's totally beside the point!"

"Is it?" Tammy demanded. "Because I'm not gonna let you wallow around in bed feeling sorry for yourself over this."

"I'm not feeling sorry for myself!"

Yes, you are.

Tammy grabbed my hand, forcing me to look up at her. "Kara, running away from this isn't going to fix anything. You can't hide away forever. When I first got here, I was terrified, but you made me feel welcome." Her eyes softened. "You made me feel like this was my home, too. You've been nothing but kind to me. So please, for the love of God, let me take care of *you* for a change."

RONAN

I had my mind made up.

Even though I was walking through town alone, my heart was racing a mile a minute in my chest. I didn't know what lay ahead of me on the other side of the creek; from the look on Kara's face the last time I'd seen her, I was guessing there'd be a whole load of pain and rejection.

But I had to try. I had to know for sure, if she'd forgive me, or if it was too late.

If she never wanted to see me again, she'd have to tell me that to my face.

Buoyed up by the thought that, either way, I would at least see her again, I felt a new spring in my step as I made my way into the center of town. Kit's pep talk had done the job. I took a deep breath, inhaling the forest air gratefully.

A sharp voice from the steps of the meeting house made me stop in my tracks.

"Ronan." Elder Frey stood with his arms crossed, staring me down. "Where are you going?"

A sharp prickle ran along the back of my neck. My hackles began to rise, and I tamped them down before I did anything stupid like snap back at him.

"I have business to attend to," I said shortly, striding onwards. "I don't know when I'll return."

"I was hoping to speak to you, Ronan." He unfolded his arms and started down the steps. "Inside."

"It'll have to wait."

"No, I don't think it can."

I stopped. *What did he mean?* In a flash, Elder Frey had crossed over to me and laid a hand on my arm. I shrugged it off.

We met each other's eyes for a long moment, my steel gaze clashing against his steady, severe countenance.

Eventually, I pushed past him and strode toward the meeting house. "Whatever it is," I said with a snarl, "make it quick."

He followed me inside without another word.

By the time we were ensconced inside the tiny office on the upper floor, my skin was itching with impatience. I'd made a decision. I needed to find my mate, to fight for her. Everything else was an unnecessary distraction, and my shifter was growing more restless with every second that passed.

The Elder sat at the desk, and I dropped down into the chair opposite. All of a sudden, I felt thirteen years old again, about to be told off by my father.

"Well?" I bristled. "What is it?"

The Elder heaved a deep sigh. There was a strange, calculating look in his pale blue eyes that I didn't like one bit.

"I'm sorry that it's come to this, Ronan." He folded his hands together. With another sigh, he pulled some papers out of the lower drawer in the desk and slid them over to me. "But you've given me no choice."

My eyes darted over the writing. The more I read, the more my stomach sank, leaving a hollow pit in its place.

"What is this?" I asked, my eyes darting up. My head was lowered in challenge, and I forced myself to straighten up, to feign indifference.

I could tell that he wasn't buying my forced pose one bit.

He tilted his head. The look on his face made me feel like I was a troublesome insect he couldn't squash. "I always knew that you would never make an Alpha."

I opened my mouth, but he continued on like he barely noticed me sitting there.

"We use the bloodline as our guide, of course. And nine times out of ten, it's right. The mantle of Alpha passes from one generation to the next, uninterrupted. Strength begets strength, strong leaders make strong heirs, and so on and so forth." His mouth twisted in contemplation. "But sometimes... it fails. Sometimes, there's a weak link."

I was frozen in place. Every word he spoke fueled the hot ball of rage inside my chest, but I couldn't find the words to counter him.

"Your father didn't believe it, at first. The memory of your mother, it softened him." Absently, Elder Frey turned his attention to the rafters above us, to the claw marks from Alphas gone by. Generations of my ancestors had carved themselves into history, right above our heads. "I spent years persuading him of the truth. That your brother was the better—the stronger—choice. Friendly, amiable, eager to please. Given time, I knew I could mold him into something truly great."

"You wanted a puppet, you mean," I spat out. The mention of Kit had shaken me back into speech. "Someone who would listen to your every word."

Elder Frey leaned forward across the desk. A thin smile lingered on his face. "We'll never know, will we? He hero-worshipped you from the start. His perfect older brother... no matter how arrogant you were, you could do no wrong in his eyes. I knew that there was no way he would ever betray you."

A spark of warmth glowed in my chest despite the curl of bitterness in the Elder's voice.

You got that right.

"We look out for each other." I glowered at the man opposite me. "It's called *loyalty*. It seems you're unfamiliar with the concept."

The Elder laughed, but there was no joy in the sound. It was harsh and cold, and I had to fight not to flinch back from it. "Loyalty? I didn't see much loyalty on the day of your Alpha ceremony. You shamed your father's memory, Ronan, by running off. That day, I knew I was right. You could never step into his shoes."

His face darkened further. "And then you returned, just in time to meet our *dear* visitors from the Bane Clan." His expression twisted; he looked unrecognizable. It was like a stranger occupied the chair, instead of the man I'd known my whole life. "Their Alpha's mate, that Bane idiot, and his whore companion."

I was out of my chair so fast I barely registered moving at all. I loomed over the Elder, hands clenched into fists. I wanted to punch the smug look off his face for daring to use that term about Kara. The urge was almost overwhelming, and I fought to get my breathing under control and quell the red mist that rose up.

"You do not—*ever*—use that language in relation to Kara."

"Or what? You'll hurt me?" Elder Frey rolled his eyes.

A growl erupted out of my chest. "She is my *mate*. You will not disrespect her."

"When I realized that you were fated for each other, I must admit, I was worried." Elder Frey chuckled. "But she was so meek, so afraid! No strength, no passion in her. Hardly a fitting mate for an Alpha. Even my attempts to drive her away, to make her see the truth, were wasted. She was as blinded to your faults as the rest of them."

The words were the final straw. With an angry roar, I lunged over the desk and hauled him up by the collar. His eyes glittered with triumph as they stared into mine.

"You don't know a damn thing about that woman," I said. "You're the one who's blind, you old fool."

Elder Frey laughed. Through the haze of anger, something in his words stuck out to me.

Even my attempts to drive her away...

"What the hell did you do to her?" I shook him, senseless with rage. "If you hurt her, I'll kill you."

"Why would I hurt her?" He wrenched himself free, straightening up. "I didn't need to. You managed to hurt her all by yourself. You might have killed Jaime in combat, but your mate is long gone."

At the mention of Jaime, something twinged in the back of my head. Slowly, I looked up to meet those cold eyes.

"You let him in. *You* brought him inside the gates," I whispered. "Didn't you?"

When he didn't respond, my voice rose up into a roar. *"Didn't you?"*

"I'll admit it." Elder Frey's lip curled. "You surprised me, Ronan. Jaime was easy enough to persuade. He was hungry for power, and the honor of leadership. I expected you to go down without a fight. Maybe you have some of your father in you, after all."

He shoved the papers in my direction. "I think we're done here."

I glanced down at the document before me. The opening sentences chilled me to the core.

I, Ronan Thornwood, do hereby relinquish my right to the position of Alpha of the Thornwood Clan.

"What is this?" I hissed.

"Sign it," he snapped. "You've poisoned this pack enough. Step aside, Ronan. Go and live like the outcast you were born to be."

I picked up the document. "If I sign this, my claim dies with me."

Elder Frey's voice turned soft, persuasive. "It won't trouble you again. Or your children, or your children's children. It's a fresh start, Ronan. You should take it. Think about Kit. What would he want?"

I looked up at him, making sure I had his full attention.

Then I ripped the paper in half, clean down the middle. The pieces fluttered down onto the desk.

"You forgot the most important part of being an Alpha. Nobody tells you how to live your life." I loomed over him. This time, I was gratified to note that he actually began to look afraid. "And *nobody* threatens your family and gets away with it."

I spared him one final, dismissive look, before heading for the door.

"Running away again?" he called after me. "Or are you worried you'll lose to an old man?"

I paused in the doorframe.

"When I get back," I said, my voice low and dangerous, "you'll be long gone. I will not allow you to set foot in Thornwood territory for the rest of your days. I'm not sparing your life out of *mercy*. Your exile will be punishment enough, after I make sure the other clans know of your treachery. No one will take you in. You don't deserve the dignity of an Alpha's challenge. You are nothing."

If he said anything in reply, I didn't hear it.

I was already out of the door.

KARA

I clutched my jacket around me and shivered. The wind blowing through the trees had grown cool, and the dark clouds overhead told me that thunder was on its way. I'd spent a long time with the Thornwoods. The peak of summer was long gone, and fall was fast approaching.

"I don't like this," Reid said.

He had been the hardest one to convince, having not warmed to

Ronan on their first and only encounter, but he'd accepted my choice to return in the end.

"I know." I gave him a quick hug. "I'm sorry. I'll see you soon, okay? All of you."

Allara's face broke into a smile. Careful not to jostle the sleeping baby in her arms, she wrapped one arm around my shoulders and squeezed.

"You got this," she whispered in my ear. "Good luck."

When she pulled away, we regarded each other for a moment. It didn't matter how many years passed, or what was going on in our lives: Allara always brought out that shy teenager in me, slightly in awe of her feisty best friend.

We were standing at the edge of the forest. I'd said my goodbyes to Jason and Tammy already. I was ready to go. After all, I had little more than the clothes I stood up in.

Most of what I need is in Thornwood territory.

My heart, for one thing. I couldn't ignore it for a moment longer. I had to find Ronan and tell him how I truly felt.

I was done being angry, or afraid.

With one final smile for my friends, I turned away and walked into the trees. I had a full day's hike ahead of me, but I wanted to do it this way. I didn't want to turn up with Reid or Allara. As much as I loved them, this was my journey to make alone.

The thick canopy of trees overhead protected me from the rain as it started to patter, soft and light, through the leaves. I tilted my head up as I strode onwards, oddly comforted by the gentle sound.

Soon, the downpour was coming thick and fast. The foliage still protected me from the worst of it, but by the time I neared the edge of Bane territory, where it abutted Thornwood land, my hair was damp and curling at the ends and I was pretty much soaked through.

Once, Ronan had told me that it didn't matter to him what I looked like, that it didn't change his feelings for me one bit.

I guess it's time to test that theory.

As I neared the creek that formed the border between territories, trepidation set in. What if I was wrong, and he really didn't want me back? What if, in my quick rush to anger that day we fought, I had destroyed what we had, once and for all?

There was no turning back now.

I didn't know what waited for me on the other side of the river.

My future, bright and glittering with possibility? Or a heartbreak so devasting I would never recover from it?

Only time would tell.

I took a deep breath as the trees around me started to thin out. It wasn't as dark here; bright patches of sunlight pierced the forest floor around my feet. The rain was still falling, but the clouds overhead were starting to clear.

I stepped out of the trees. I'd reached the creek.

On the other side, Thornwood territory stretched for miles. I shivered. Once again, I was a stranger in these lands.

He won't hurt me. No matter what.

Not physically, anyway. My heart would be in pieces if this didn't work.

The creek was at its widest point here. The shallow waters swirled at ankle height, and large stones littered the crossing, forming a natural bridge.

I hopped onto the first one easily enough. I looked up at the opposite side, toward my destination. Through the rain, everything in sight glittered with refracted sunlight.

My heart caught in my chest when a hazy figure came into view.

I took another step, keeping my eyes fixed on the man in the distance.

The clouds cleared, and a beam of sunlight fell onto his face. I just about stopped breathing.

Ronan.

His gaze was intense, piercing. Even from this distance, the light in his amber eyes took my breath away.

He strode easily from rock to rock, like he'd done it a thousand times before. I was less graceful. Nerves and impatience churned in my gut, and more than a couple of times I slipped on a damp stone surface.

By the time we reached the middle of the creek, I was trembling with anticipation. I put a foot wrong, and almost fell headlong into the river. He caught me around the waist.

"Kara," he said, his eyes drinking me in. "What are you doing out here?"

I bit my lip. Now that the moment had come, the words stuck in my throat. I closed my eyes briefly, and swallowed down my nerves. "I wanted—"

I reached up and tangled my fingers in his hair. The touch sent a shock of electricity down my arm. It had barely been two days since I'd seen him, but it felt like a lifetime. It felt unbelievably good, being able to put my hands on him again.

"Why are *you* here?" I asked.

He was still holding me close, and I curled my hands around his forearms. I pulled back, looking him in the eye.

"I was coming to get *you*." His eyes blazed. It might have been the light, but for a brief flicker, I thought I saw his shifter rise up from their depths. "I've come to take you home, Kara. Come home with me."

The way he spoke was simple, and appeared as easy as breathing to him. I leaned into the seductive promise of him, closing my eyes. Warmth flooded through my chest, and I forgot about everything else. Nothing mattered, only the sunlight on my back, the rain on my face, and the feel of Ronan's arms around me, our chests pressed close. His heart beat against mine.

"Are you sure?" I whispered.

I didn't want to ask the question. That was why I was standing here, after all: to come back. To come *home*.

Allara's pack would always accept me, but I didn't belong there anymore. My spirit longed to return with Ronan. But there was a shard of doubt still lodged in my chest, a terror that this was all too good to be true.

"It was never about a treaty," Ronan said, his voice deep with emotion. "You weren't here because of some political pact, or because I saw you as collateral. From the moment I first saw you, I wanted you with me—always."

He slid his hand up my neck, tilting my head back until my eyes met his. "*You* are my family, Kara. As much as Kit is. More, in some ways. You are my future."

I hardly dared to believe what he was saying. It was more than I hoped for. It was everything.

"What are you trying to say?"

"I'm saying I want you to be my mate. Properly." He dug around inside the pocket of his shirt before pulling something out.

I squinted in the sunlight, and my heart started to hammer even harder than it already was.

"I should have done this sooner," he said. "I'm sorry."

I couldn't find the words to reply.

He held the ring between his thumb and forefinger, fumbling for my hand. The metal was warm to the touch from having lain against his chest. "Kara, this has been in my family for... I don't know how long. It's a human tradition I know... but I want you to have it." I could only nod, overwhelmed, as he slid the ring onto my ring finger. "It's a promise."

The ring was gold, two hands linked by a heart. I ran my thumb over the design, and tears blurred my eyes.

"It's beautiful," I murmured. "It's *perfect.*"

A smile lingered around the corners of his mouth as he took my face in his broad hands and pressed a soft kiss to my lips. The second our mouths met, I felt the same rush as I did the first time. Every moment with Ronan was fresh and new and exhilarating. It only lasted a second before he pulled away, and I bit down a sigh of frustration.

"The life of an Alpha's mate won't be easy," he said, absently tucking a strand of hair behind my ear.

I leaned into the touch before his words fully registered.

"Hang on…did you say, *Alpha*?"

"I'm done hiding from this, Kara." His expression shifted, turning serious. "It's who I am. It's time to stop worrying about living up to someone else's expectations and start making my own."

I tilted my head. "Why did you run away from the pack, Ronan? I need to know."

He pinched the bridge of his nose, and sighed. "Um… I don't have a good reason."

"Tell me anyway," I said. "And I'll never bring it up again. I promise. I just want to understand why."

He nodded. "I… my father had made it clear since I was pretty young that I wouldn't be a good Alpha. That I just didn't have it in me to lead. He said it constantly, in fact. That's why they had Kit, I think. So that there would be a second heir to inherit the title. But Dad died earlier than expected, and Kit just isn't old enough… so they told me I had to take on the mantle. I felt like a fraud, stepping in to take something away from my brother, when everyone knew I couldn't do the job well. I couldn't handle the judgment from the pack. From Elder Frey…" Ronan shook his head and *tsked* loudly. "But I couldn't leave. That would have left the pack vulnerable. I ran out of the compound, got about a hundred yards down the road, then turned back. I couldn't leave my pack unguarded. What if something had happened to one of them? I would never have been able to forgive myself."

"Damn," I said faintly. "You really are an Alpha, aren't you, protecting the pack even then."

He laughed suddenly, smiling down at me. "I… I suppose I am. I never thought of it that way, before. I just figured it was one more thing I couldn't do right, only half-running off, and not letting Kit get on with it."

Then he grew serious once more. "Are you okay with that? With me being an Alpha?" Ronan's brow furrowed as a sudden spark of concern entered his eyes. "You didn't sign up for any of this."

"Neither did you. Ronan..." I couldn't hold back my smile any longer. "I'm proud of you."

Ronan shot a crooked smile back at me. "You came out here, all this way, by yourself..."

"For you," I finished for him, in a rush. I took his hands in mine and stood on my tiptoes to kiss him properly. When I pulled away, we were both breathing heavily. "I know the life of an Alpha and his mate, all the responsibility... it's not what either of us pictured, but that doesn't have to be a bad thing. Maybe we can figure it out together."

I shrieked as he hitched me into the air, and my legs scrabbled for purchase around his waist. He didn't seem fazed, just pressed burning kisses against my cheeks, my neck, my nose, and forehead.

I submitted to the attention, laughing, before drawing him into a proper kiss.

By the time we walked back together to the village, hand in hand, we were both soaked from head to toe.

I couldn't have cared less.

EPILOGUE

KARA

Ronan straightened and brushed off his hands. He was grinning from ear to ear, and I couldn't help but grin back at him.

"That's the last one." He stared down at the pile of wood at his feet. Here and there, pieces of barbed wire glinted, poking through the long grass. "Time to start building another bonfire, I reckon."

I wanted to take him to task about the barbed wire—someone was going to slice themselves up if they weren't careful—but Ronan looked so happy I couldn't bear to dampen my mood.

The project had been a couple of weeks in the making. The plan had been to pull everything to the ground at first, but then it was agreed that one of the watchtowers should stay.

But the fences were gone, at long last.

The open forest stood around us. Pack members wandered past us in a daze, staring like they couldn't believe their eyes. After years of being penned in, they were free to roam their whole pack territory to their heart's content.

It was like Ronan had said, getting up to the platform to speak after our bonding ceremony.

You can't protect the ones you love from danger by hiding away from the world. Danger is out there, but it's our bonds with each other that will keep us safe. The forest is our home, our territory. We won't be cut off from it any longer.

The applause was the loudest I'd ever heard. The pack had rallied around Ronan in his decision, just like I'd hoped they would.

Allara came to stand beside me. She was holding a beer, and a soft smile played at the corners of her mouth. Reid's foster mother was looking after the baby in honor of the occasion. It was nice to see my best friend get the chance to let her hair down a little.

"Thank you," she said, tilting the neck of her bottle in my direction.

I blinked. "Uh... you're welcome?" I narrowed my eyes at her. "What did I do, exactly?"

"Exactly what I asked you to do." Her voice was soft. "You've helped to unite the Bane and Thornwood Clans. Because of you, we don't have to fear them. Your children will be our kin."

I opened my mouth, then closed it. I ducked my head, heat flooding my cheeks. "I hadn't thought about it like that. I just..."

"Fell in love," Allara finished for me, smirking.

"Shut up." I nudged her with my elbow. "Wait, did you plan this?"

Allara scoffed. "Don't be stupid. I couldn't have known! I couldn't go with Reid, and I needed someone to go in my place. Simple." It might have been a trick of the light, but I could've sworn that she winked at me. "Maybe I was *hoping* you'd find a match along the way."

Allara the matchmaker. I shook my head, dumbfounded.

"Anyway, it all worked out in the end," she said happily. "Now all we have to do is get those two to behave themselves."

She pointed toward Ronan and Reid, where they were dragging one of the fence posts in from the edge of the woods. It was a huge log, the size of a tree trunk. Both men were having an intense debate about the best way to carry it, but they kept waving off anyone who tried to come over and help shoulder some of the weight.

I sighed. "I think I preferred it when they were locking horns."

Allara snorted into her drink. "Agreed. They're a liability like this, I swear. They're going to lead each other into mischief."

"Well, we'll just have to lead them straight back out of it, won't we?"

She laughed, and shot me a look filled with respect.

We watched idly for a while. Ronan brushed his burnished hair out of his eyes in a gesture that had become achingly familiar. The sun was low in the sky, and his eyes, always striking, were particularly vibrant in the evening light. His eyes met mine, and his features softened. The change was only slight—nobody noticed but me—but it was enough to send a spark of warmth through my chest.

The tang of fall was in the air. Dead leaves crunched underfoot, and debris from the old fences littered the ground around us. A cool, fresh wind rippled through the trees, and blue smoke began to rise behind the rooftops ahead of us.

Allara linked her arm through mine and raised her beer. "Here's to..." She tilted her head at me. "What?"

I smiled as the sound of laughter reached me. The sound of family, of home. My hand slid down to my still-flat belly, where my child grew. The next Alpha of the Thornwood Clan.

I clinked my bottle of water against her beer. "Here's to beginnings."

AMELIA SHAW

THE END

164

BABY OF THE WOLF SNEAK PEEK

~

Read on for a sneak peek of:

Baby of the Wolf

Book 4 in the 'Pack Loyalty' series

~

CHAPTER 1
AMY

The morning that stick turned blue two years ago, I didn't celebrate like other expectant mothers may have. I turned around and vomited into the toilet bowl, for the third time that morning.

I'd been sick for weeks but hadn't thought much of it, putting the sickness down to stress from work, or maybe a stomach bug. But when I'd added up the dates and realized I was three weeks late on my period, I'd known it was time for a test.

Pregnant. It was the last thing I'd expected to become at twenty-three and still single. I couldn't blame anyone but myself, though. And luckily, or unluckily for me depending on how you looked at it, I knew exactly who the father was. I'd fallen, or rather jumped into bed with a guy I'd met at a bar. Not exactly my style, but I hadn't been able to resist him.

Noah.

I couldn't forget him even though I'd tried. I still dreamt about him almost every night and when I look at his child, the daughter he'd made with me that night, his piercing blue eyes stare right back at me.

I shook myself out of my reverie as I walked up the two flights of stairs to my tiny apartment. It was small, but it was rent controlled, and a short walk to my parents' house which was essential, since my mom did most of the babysitting while I worked.

I put my key in the door and pushed it open. "Hello!"

"Hey Amy!" Mom called out as she walked towards me, holding my daughter in her arms. "How was your day?"

"Mama. Mama," Trixie said, leaning forward, reaching for me with her chubby hands.

I dropped my bags, the exhaustion of the day disappearing as I pulled my beautiful girl into my arms.

"Hello baby. Have you been a good girl for Grandma today?" I squeezed my daughter tight to me and kissed the golden curls on her head. "Thanks for looking after her, Mom."

"No problem," Mom said, reaching for her bag which sat on the small table by the front door. "I put some soup on the stove and did some washing. You should try to get an early night tonight. You've got circles under your eyes."

Gee, thanks.

I sighed. "Yeah. Trixie hasn't been sleeping well. She's teething again, I think."

Her cheeks would bloom bright red, and she'd cry with her hands stuck in her mouth for hours.

"I saw her canines trying to pop through her gums on both sides," Mom said, opening the front door to leave. "They're notorious for being the worst of all the teeth for pain."

Damn. I knew it.

"Thanks, Mom. See you tomorrow." I kissed her on the cheek and closed the door behind her.

I sighed, resting against the door, a bone deep tiredness washing over me. A single mom's life wasn't easy, and anyone who said so was utterly insane.

Trixie launched herself towards the ground, and I carefully set her on her feet. "Are you hungry sweetheart? Let's see what sort of soup Grandma cooked for us."

Trixie took off towards the kitchen, running at a rate reserved for kids much older than herself. She was fifteen months old, but had been walking for almost six months already.

"Oh.... pumpkin soup." I inhaled as I lifted the lid off the pot. "From scratch! Grandma is the best."

I settled into our nightly routine: dinner, clean up, bath, and then bed.

"Such a big, strong girl, aren't you?" I said while dressing Trixie for sleep, and not for the first time, noticing how muscled she was. Her arms were thick and her biceps defined.

"Mama," Trixie said, reaching for the diaper beside her and handing it to me.

"Thank you, baby."

I dressed her into her pajamas and zipped her into her toddler sleeping bag. "Bedtime, sweetheart."

I popped her down into her crib and handed her the only toy she liked to sleep with, a grey wolf that my dad had gotten her for Christmas last year. At the time I'd thought it was such a strange toy to give to a little girl, but Dad said that Trixie had picked it out of all the toys he'd offered her at the store.

He'd been right. She loved it. She wouldn't go anywhere without the grubby thing.

I stared down at her and watched as she nestled into the wolf, clenching it with her chubby little fist, then she closed her eyes.

I snuck out of her room and sighed as I closed the door behind me. She was an angel when it came to her routine. I was really blessed compared to other moms. But the likelihood of her sleeping through the night was low, so I'd better get into bed myself soon.

I walked into the kitchen and put away the rest of the soup, then flicked on the TV to relax for an hour. I deserved a little bit of adult normalcy, surely?

I hadn't stopped working since she was three months old, and I had no intentions of doing so. Trixie and I were going to survive and thrive, with a little help from my parents but not much else.

My daughter deserved the best of everything, and just because I was a young, single mom, didn't mean I couldn't provide for her. Quite the opposite. The love I had for my daughter drove me like nothing else ever had.

I was dozing off around episode two of some supernatural drama on TV when a strange, high pitched growling noise came from Trixie's bedroom.

I jumped to my feet. "What the hell?"

I bolted towards her room. Had some wild animal managed to get inside? No way!

My heart pounded in my chest as I pushed her bedroom door open. I looked around, narrowing my eyes in the dim light.

A growl sounded again, and I glanced towards the crib I crept over, icy fear trickling down my veins. *No, not my baby.*

I looked into the crib half afraid I was about to find a wild raccoon in there with her, but there was nothing abnormal going on around her. Nothing at all. Trixie was fast asleep, her wolfy clutched to her side.

The growl came again, followed by a sharp bark. I stared in horror at my daughter as her little mouth opened to make the noises that had woken me. Again and again, she barked and growled, her face contorting in her sleep as though she were fighting some fierce beast.

Oh, God. What the hell is happening to her?

I slammed both hands over my mouth so that I didn't wake her.

Instead, I just stared in disbelief as she snarled and chomped her little teeth together like she was biting something. Then she relaxed, her face clearing of any animal-like signs, and once again she was my angel, fast sleep.

I stood at her crib side, waiting for another showing of the strange animal side of my daughter, but it didn't surface again.

Exhausted beyond belief, I staggered to my own bed and crawled under the covers, tears streaking down my cheeks.

I had no idea what had just happened, but it was another thing to add to the list of things I didn't know about my baby. And unfortunately, I knew why I didn't know.

It was because so many of her traits came from her father, a man I barely knew and had no contact with. Mom had told me that I hadn't walked until I was thirteen months and was super talkative at Trixie's age. Mom described my physique as being 'Michelin man.' Dough boy soft.

My daughter was super advanced physically, and yet barely talked. She was strong and fit in a way that toddlers just shouldn't be, and now made animal barking noises in her sleep.

There was also the fact that I was certain her eyes changed colors at times. They were blue, an electric, bright blue, but I'd seen them swirl to yellow, or even silver sometimes. My mom and the doctor had told me I was crazy, and I'd never been able to get a good photo of the shift. But it was there. Something... odd.

Was that connected to her father too?

Who was Noah... really? And what did he have to do with all of this?

I closed my eyes and pictured him in my mind's eye. He was six foot three, with a body most underwear models would die for. He had a six pack so defined that I had been able to literally run my tongue around every muscle, through every groove.

The base, animal attraction between us had been so intense, it was embarrassing to admit how quickly I'd gone home with him.

Our eyes had met over the dance floor, and heat had flooded my body so fast my legs had trembled from one single glance. His blue eyes had darkened so much so that they'd appeared black by the time he stood in front of me.

A few words were spoken, and a minute later he was kissing me, pressing me into the wall behind us and making it clear for the whole room that he wanted me.

I hadn't been much better, gripping his shirt and hauling him into my aching body. I'd needed him that night, in a way I've never needed anyone before or since.

He asked me to go back to his place with him, an hour's drive into the forest.

I'd been terrified to go with him, but excited at the same time. Despite normally having pretty good common sense, with that intense, throbbing need clawing at my belly, I'd had no choice. That feeling had overridden whatever smart voice in my head had been saying 'don't go.'

I went home with him, much to my shame. And what a night it had been!

We'd arrived in a small town I'd never heard of and once getting past the massive wall and gates that seemed to be designed to keep everyone out, Noah had parked in front of his log cabin. We got up the front steps, but no further.

He took me against the wall outside the front door because neither of us had been able to go another step. We hadn't even made it inside before my first orgasm had crashed into me. But it hadn't been the last. Noah had made love to me all night, showing a stamina and level of care that I'd never experienced.

I shivered in my cold lonely bed, and the tears began to fall in earnest this time. Noah scared me, on a deep level. My need for him, and my inability to resist him, was one of the main reasons I'd stayed away.

Not to mention the shame. First of having unprotected sex with a complete stranger, then of staying away so long. And the longer I waited, the harder it became to reach out, if I could find him.

I'd never looked for him after that morning. When I woke up around dawn I'd walked to the nearest road, called an uber, and gotten back into the city without a backwards glance. I'd never gone back to the club where he'd picked me up. Never tried to find that town where he lived.

Now, I didn't think I could put off the inevitable any longer. Something was wrong with my baby girl, and I knew, in a bone deep way, that her biological father would have the answer.

I fell asleep and dreamt of my dream lover. When I awoke, I began making plans for our trip, and hoped to god I'd be able to find the town that wasn't on any map.

9 781764 127127